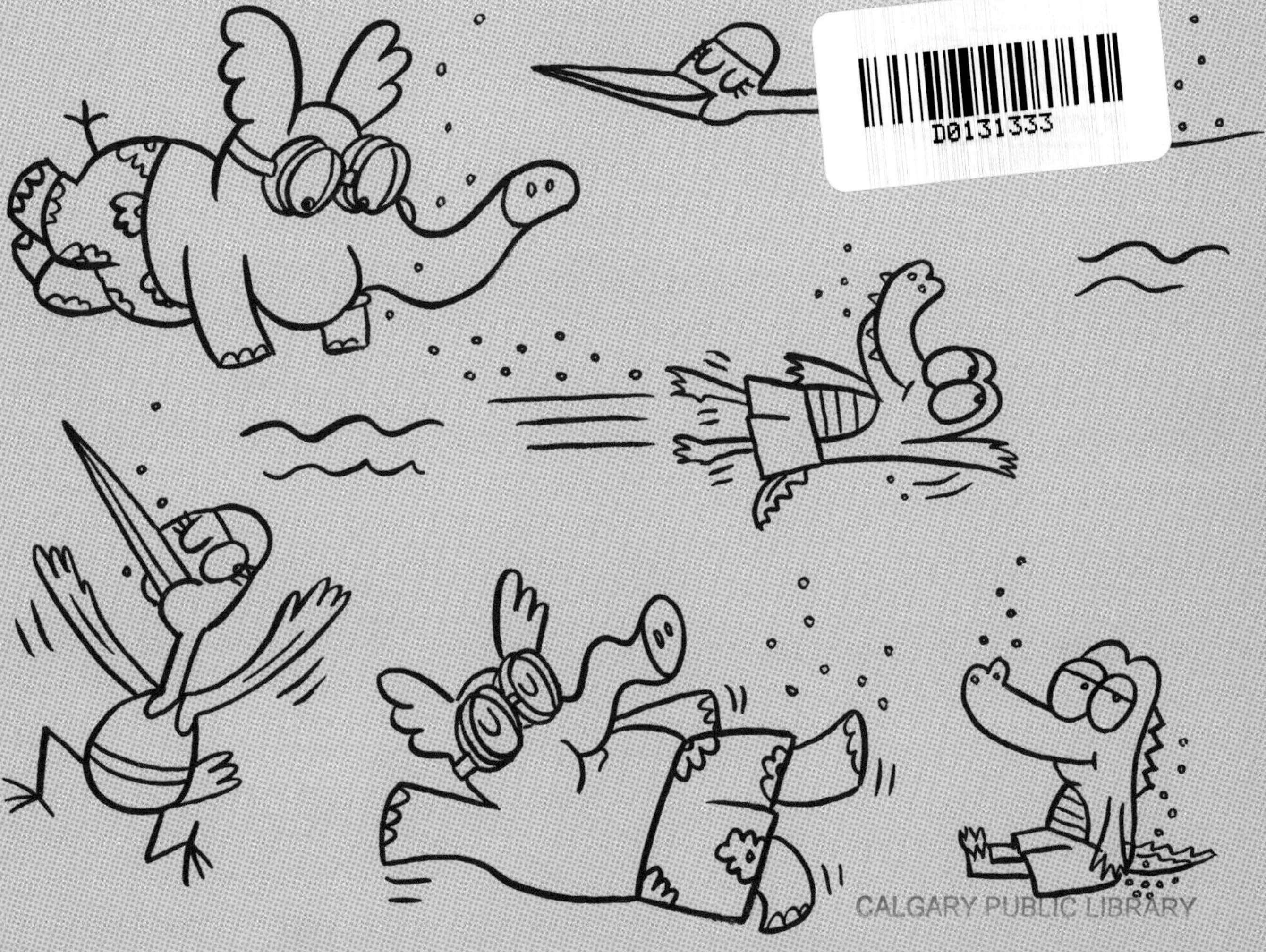

Copyright © 2012 Ethan Long
Balloon Toons® is a registered trademark of Harriet Ziefert, Inc.
All rights reserved/CIP data is available. Published in the United States 2012 by
Blue Apple Books, 515 Valley Street, Maplewood, NJ 07040
www.blueapplebooks.com
First Edition   Printed in China 03/12

HC ISBN: 978-1-60905-201-0   PB ISBN: 978-1-60905-202-7
1 2 3 4 5 6 7 8 9 10   1 2 3 4 5 6 7 8 9 10

BALLOON TOONS®

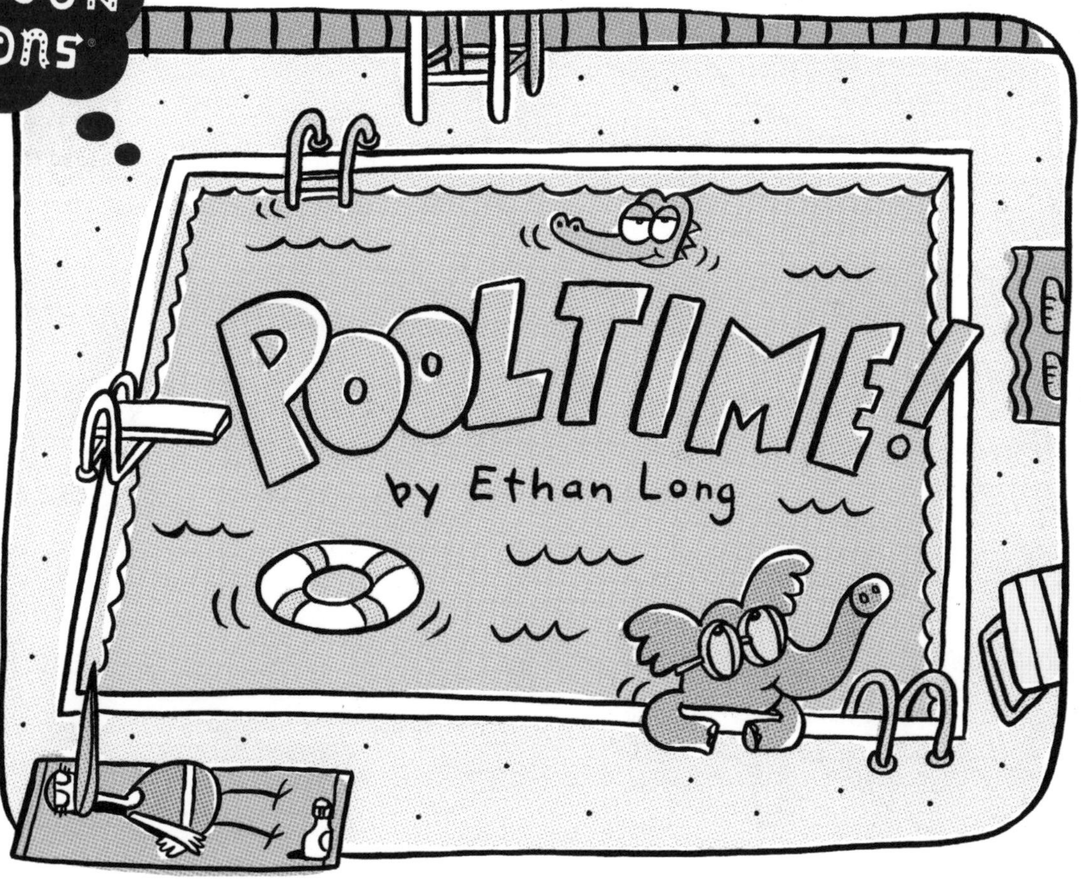
POOLTIME!
by Ethan Long

BLUE APPLE

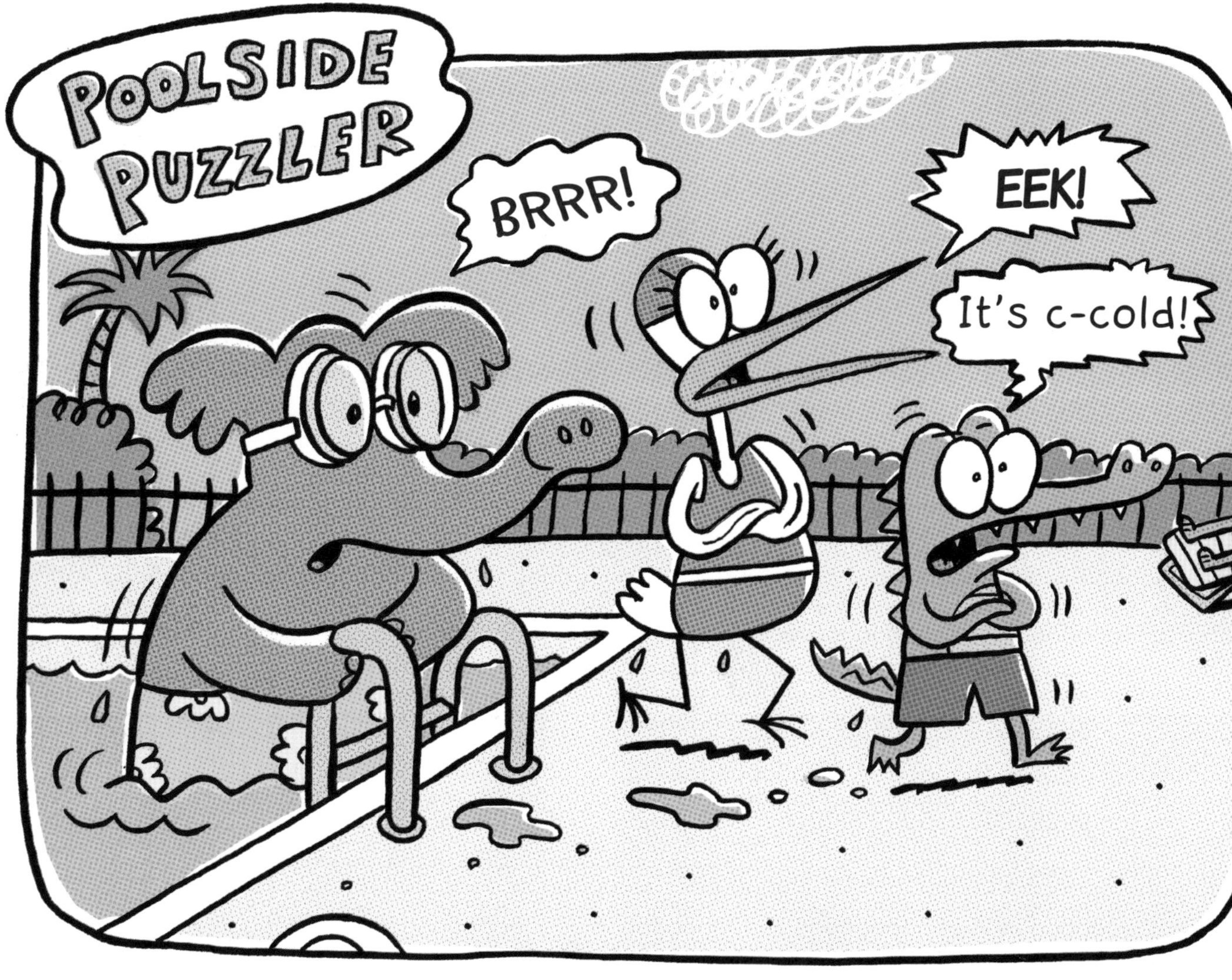
POOLSIDE PUZZLER
BRRRR!
EEK!
It's c-cold!

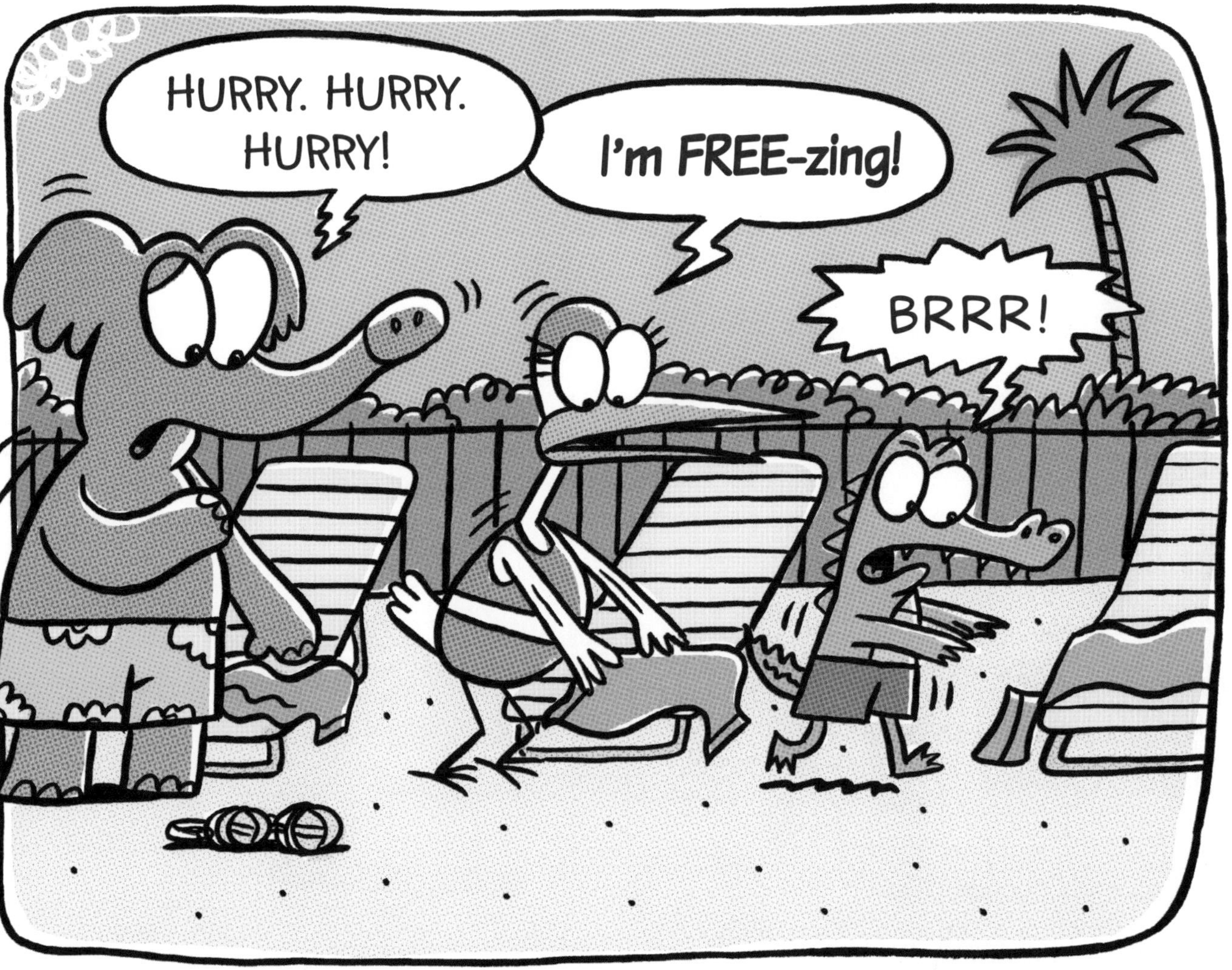
HURRY. HURRY. HURRY!
I'm FREE-zing!
BRRRR!

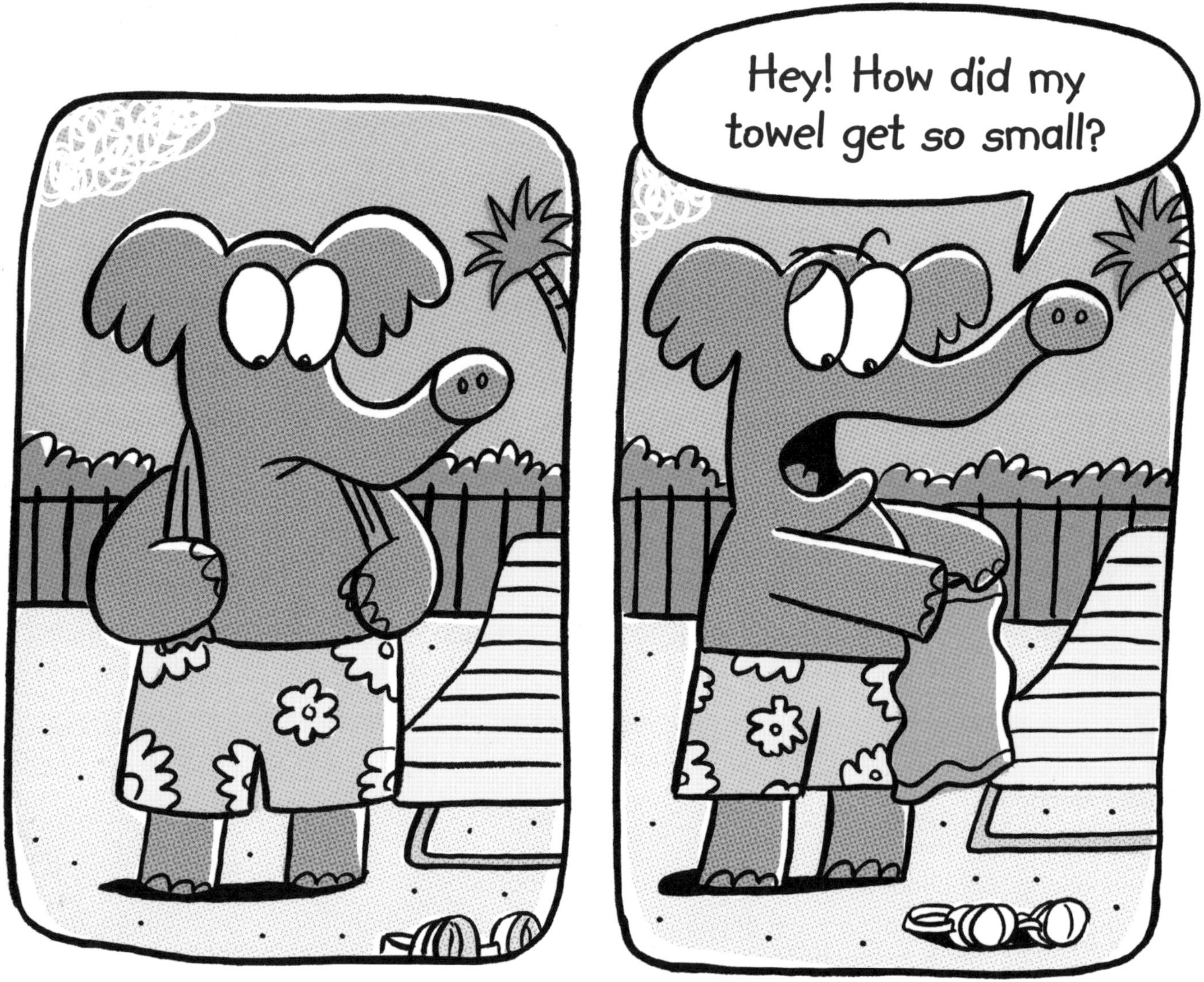
Hey! How did my towel get so small?

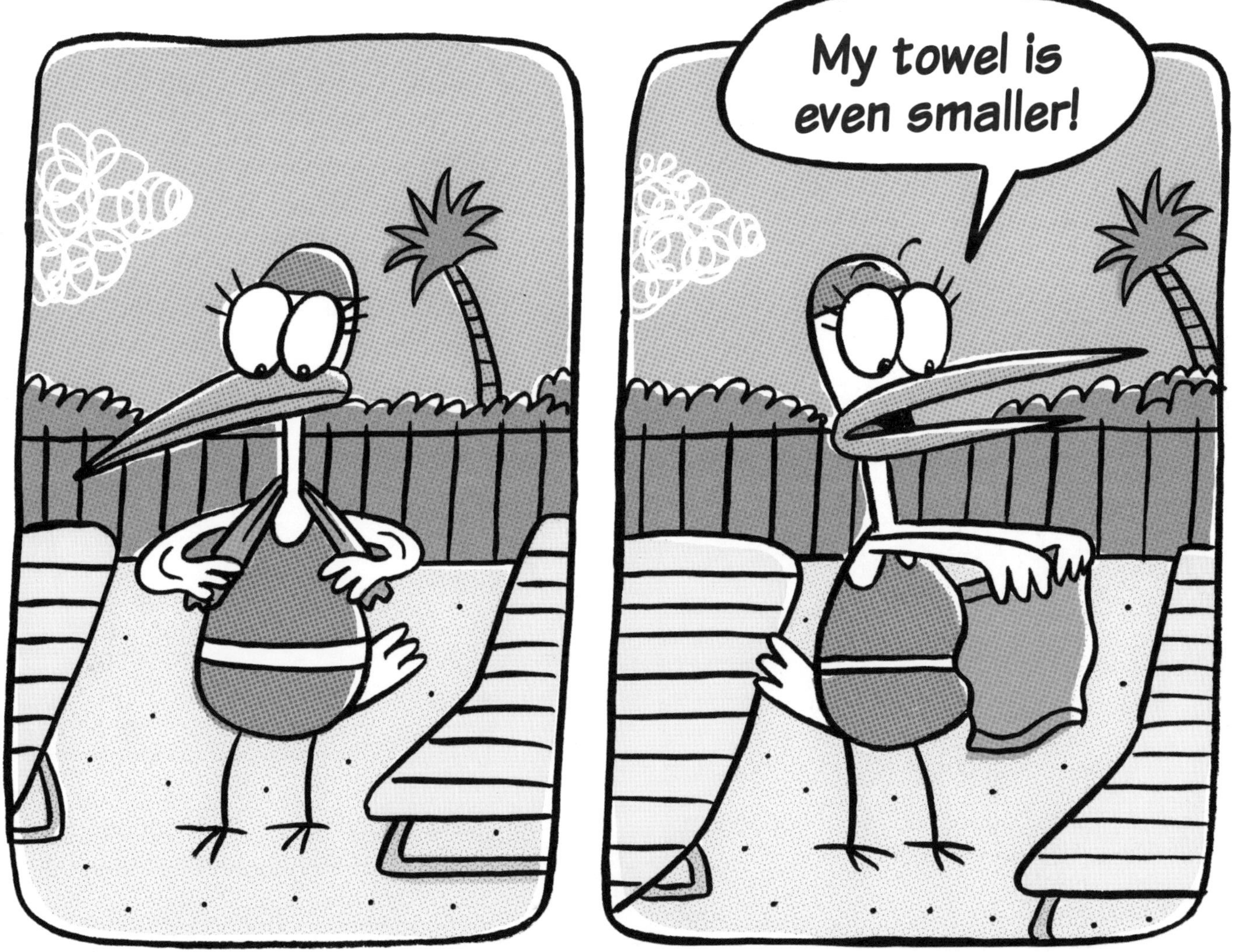
My towel is even smaller!

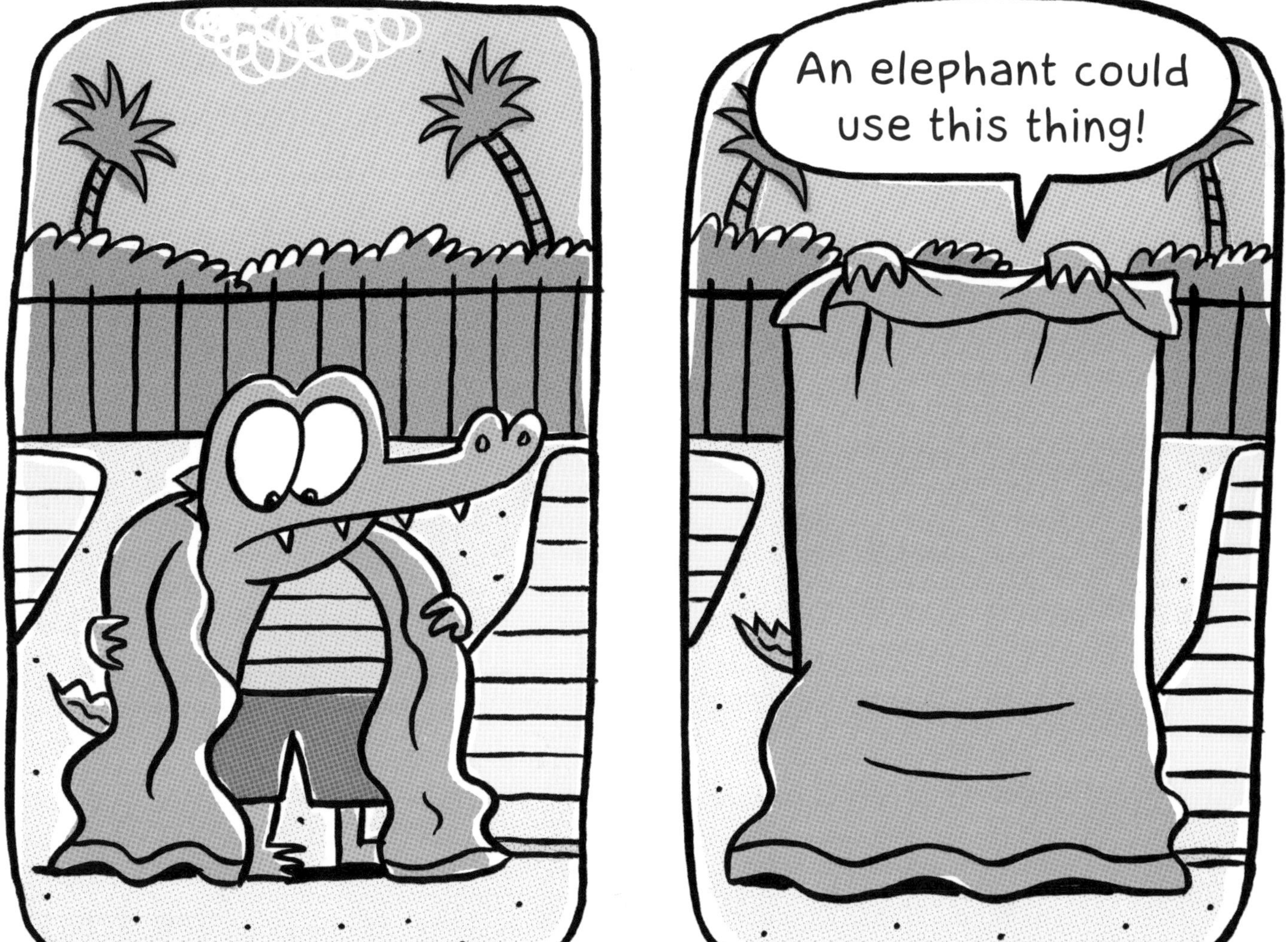
An elephant could use this thing!

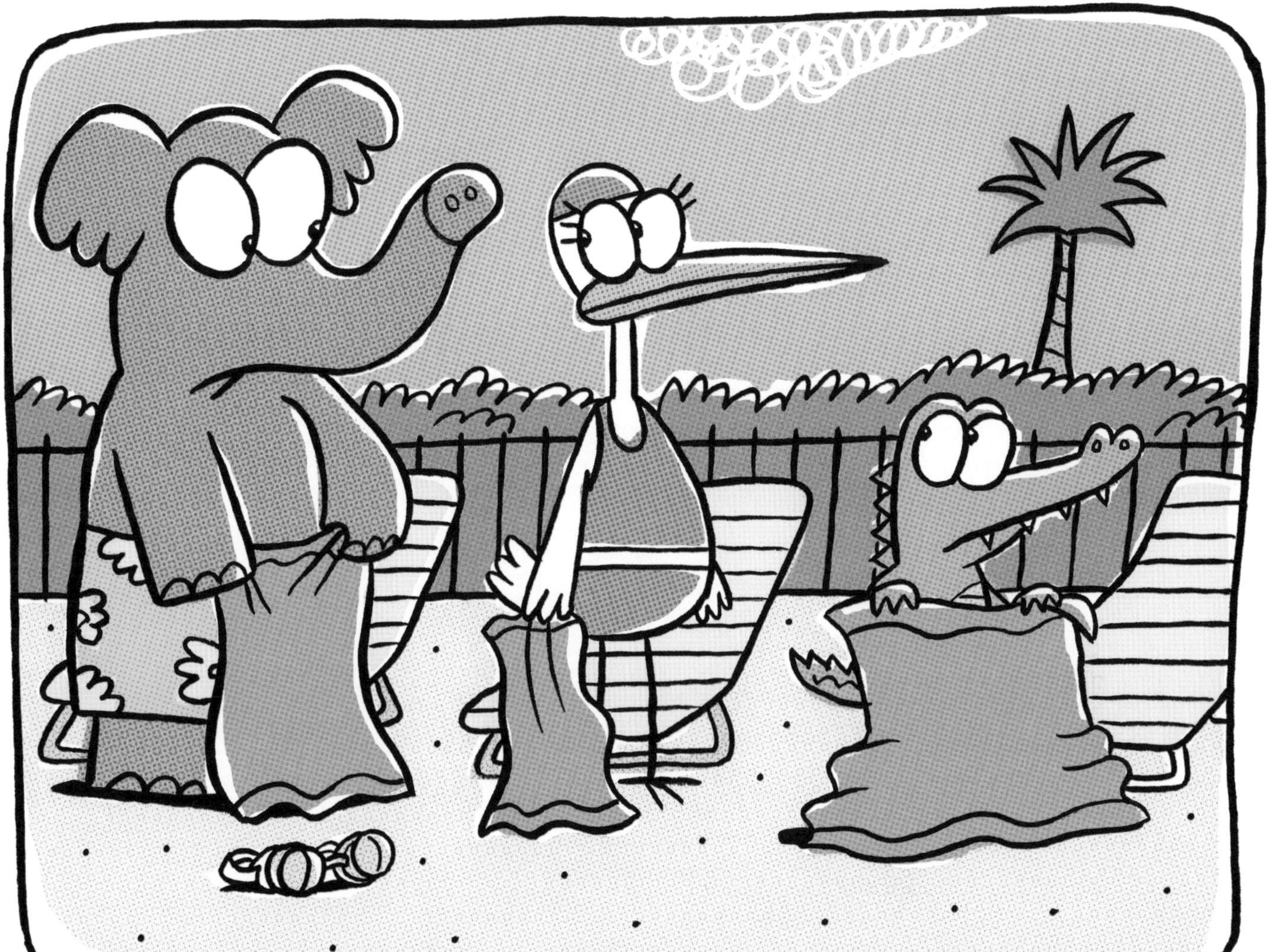

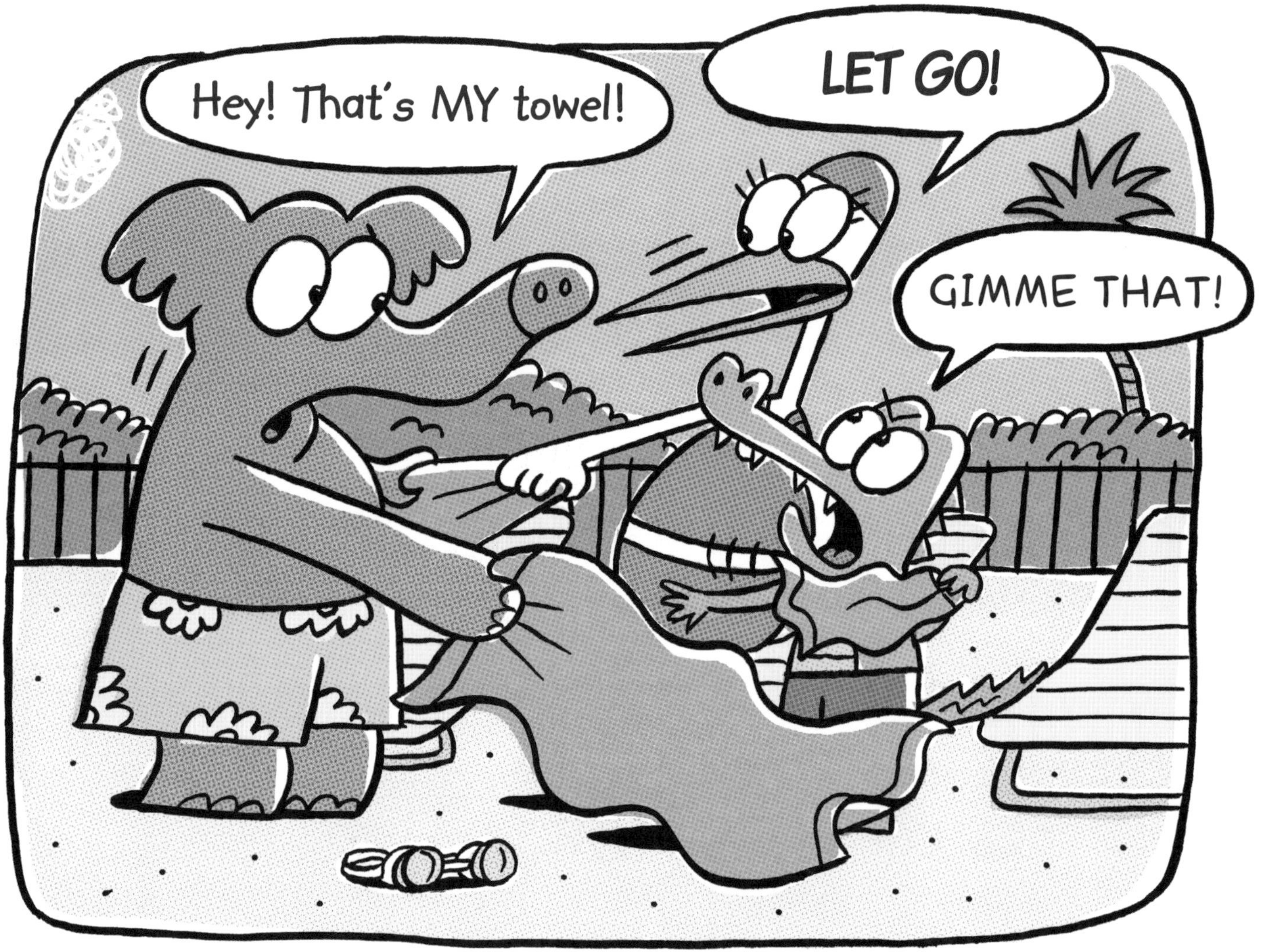
Hey! That's MY towel!
LET GO!
GIMME THAT!

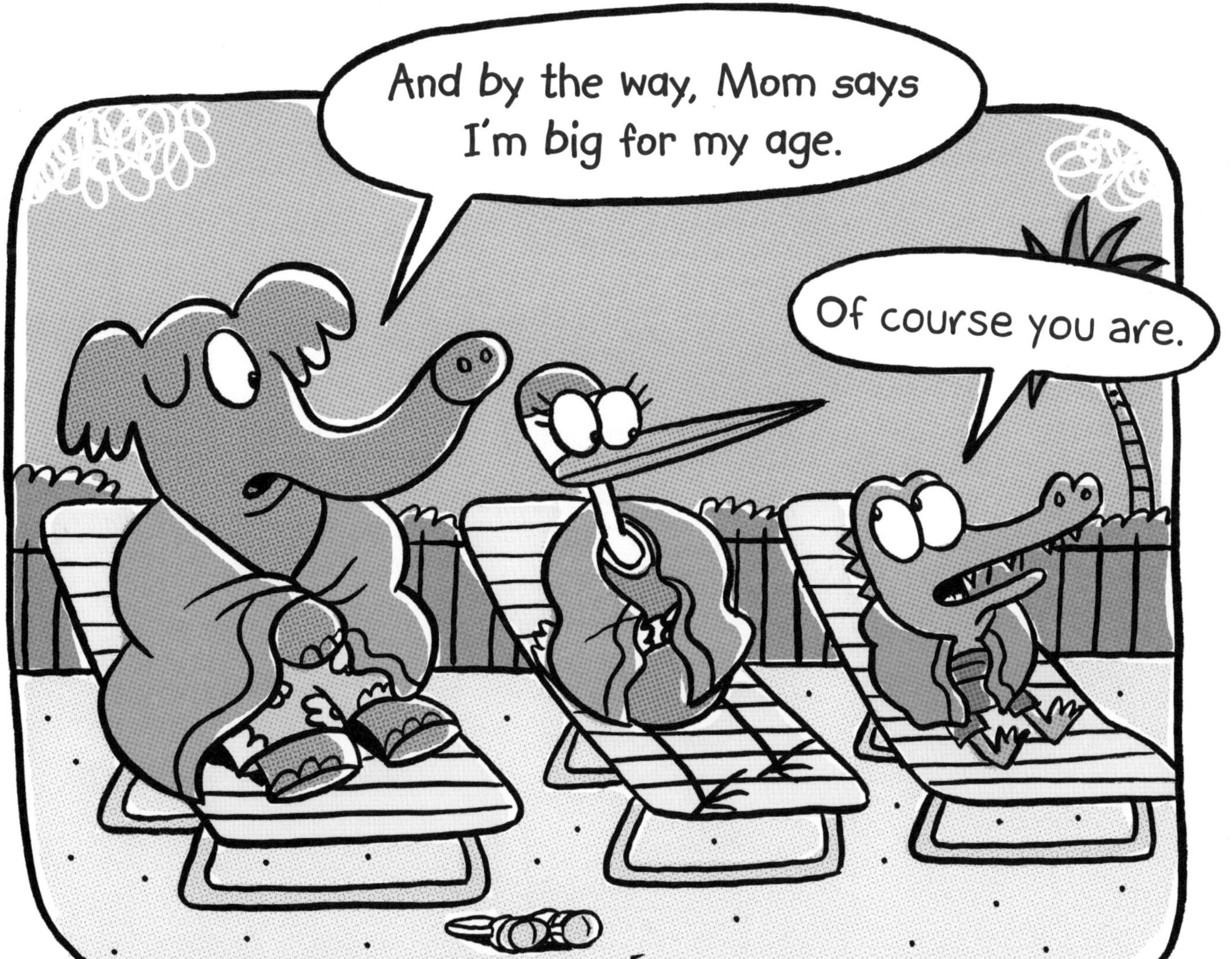
And by the way, Mom says I'm big for my age.
Of course you are.

SUMMERTIME SNACK
MENU
Soft Pretzel .50
Cotton Candy 1.00
Candy Bar .75
Ice Cream .50
Hot Dog 1.00

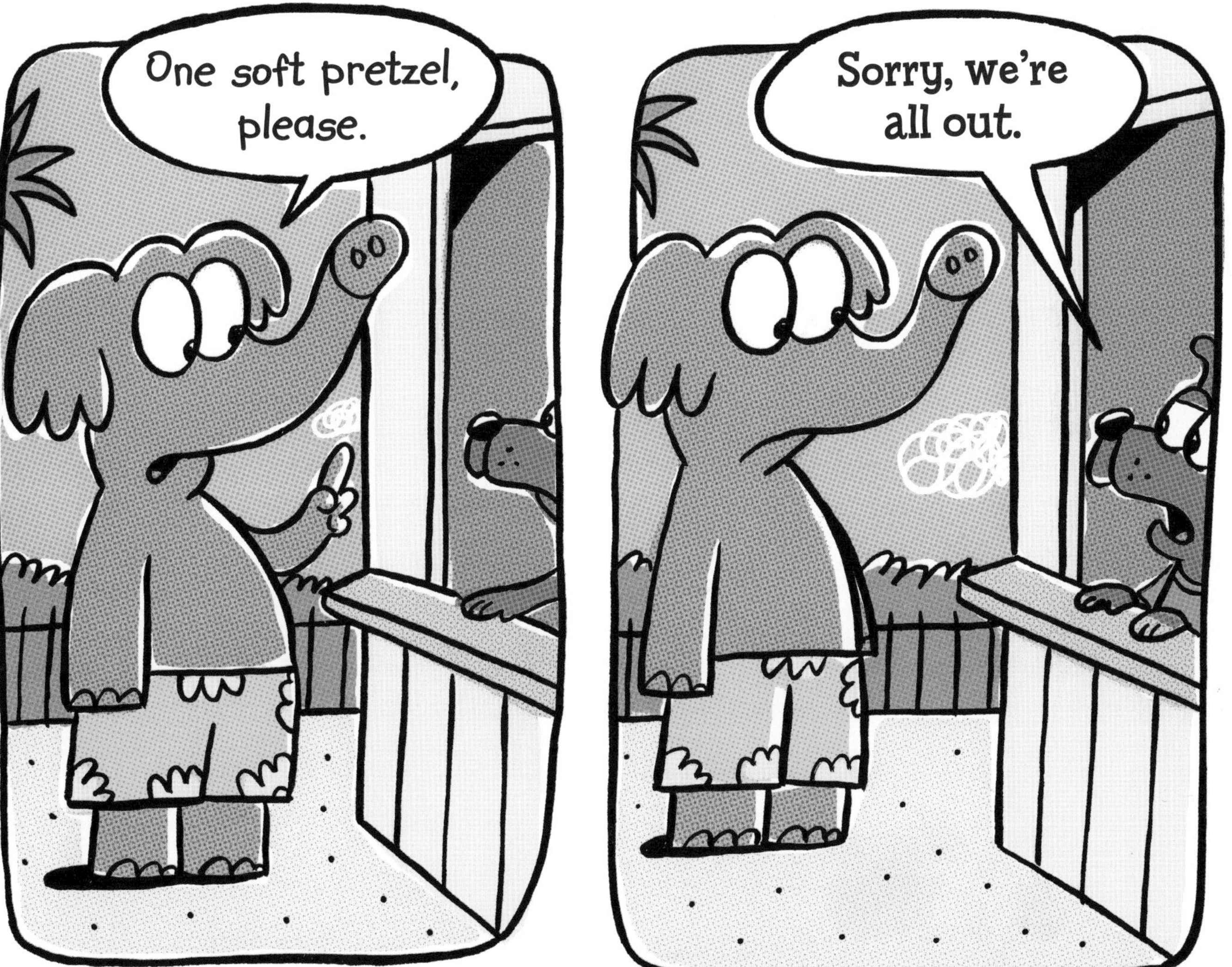
One soft pretzel, please.
Sorry, we're all out.

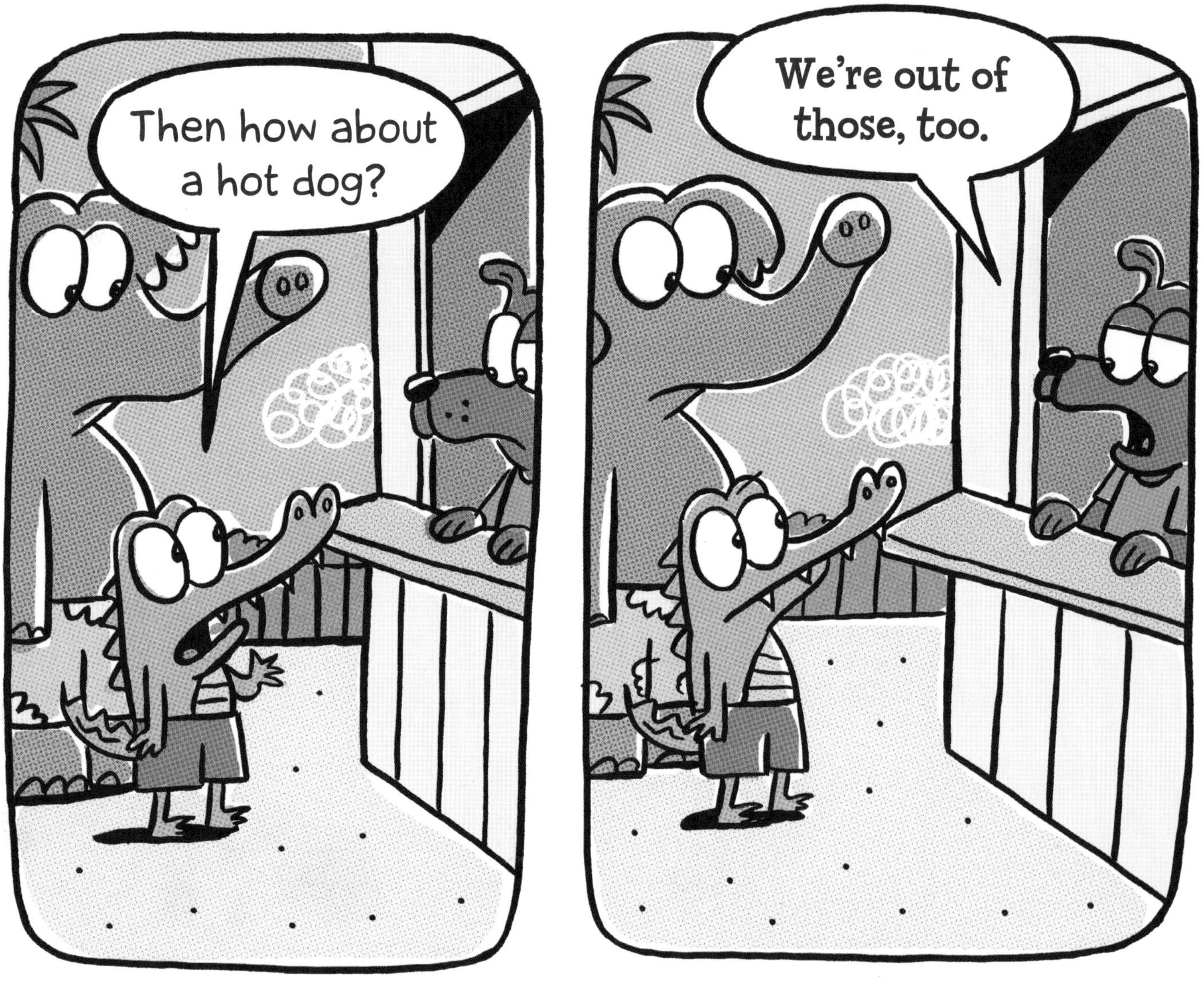
Then how about a hot dog?
We're out of those, too.

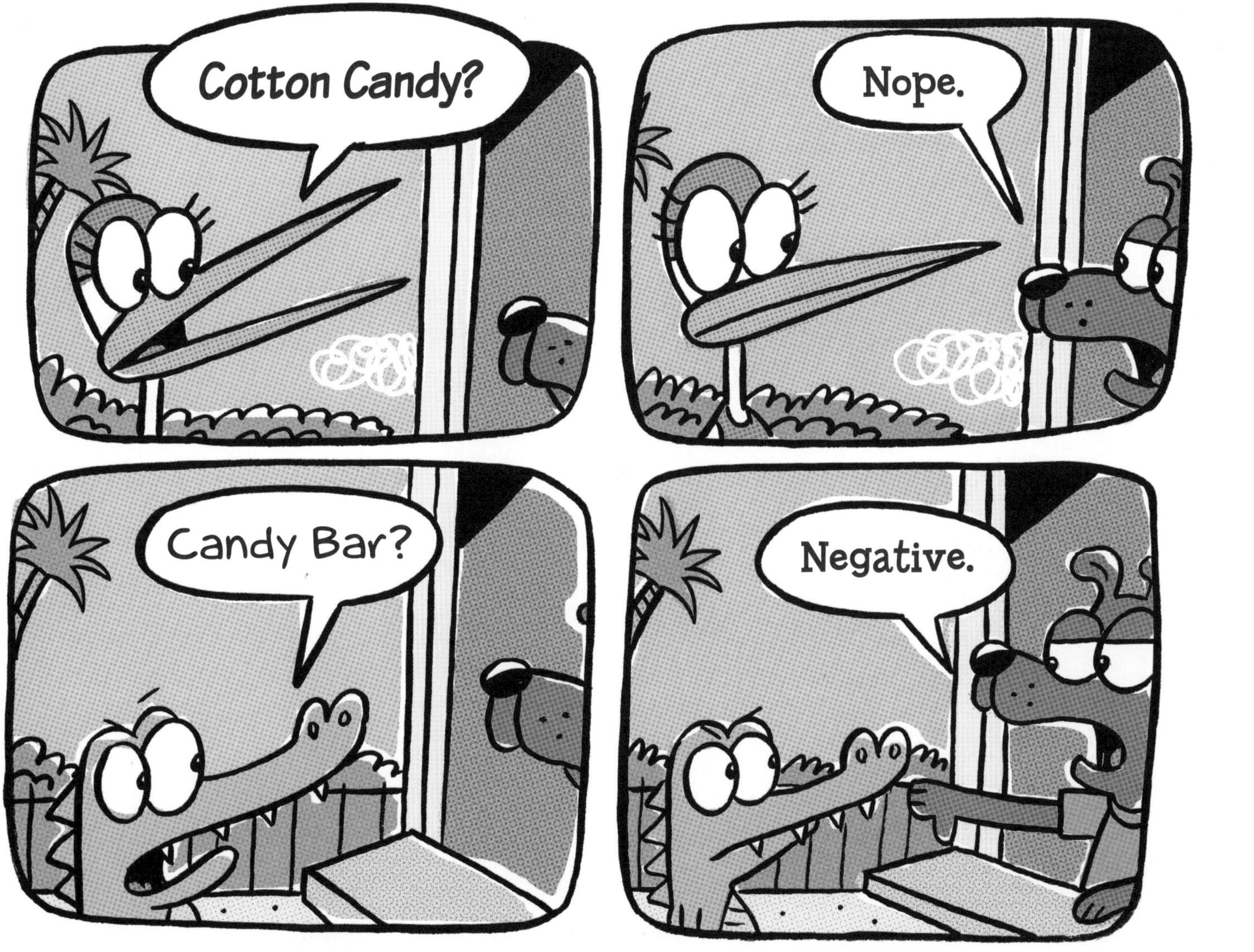
Cotton Candy?
Nope.
Candy Bar?
Negative.

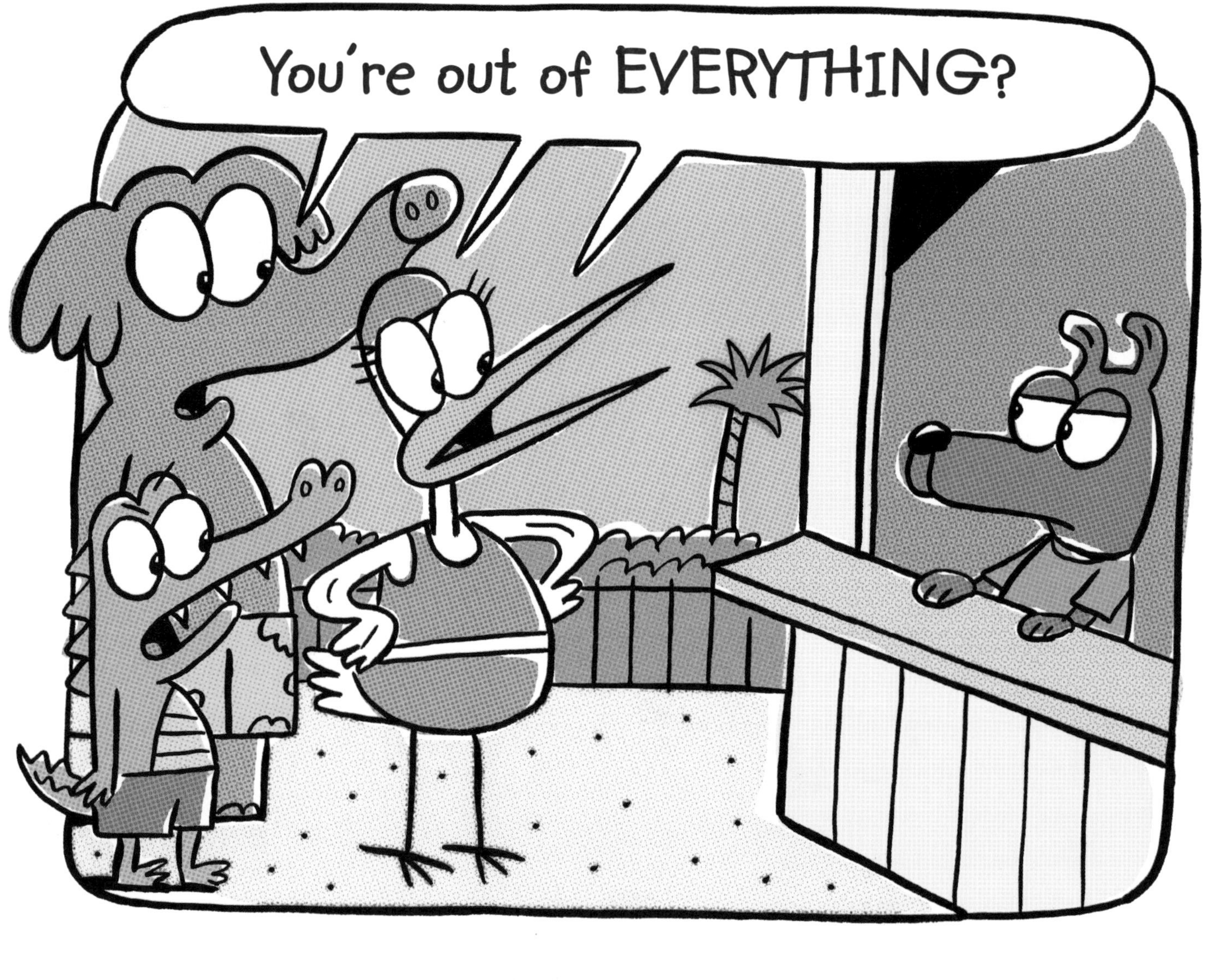
You're out of EVERYTHING?

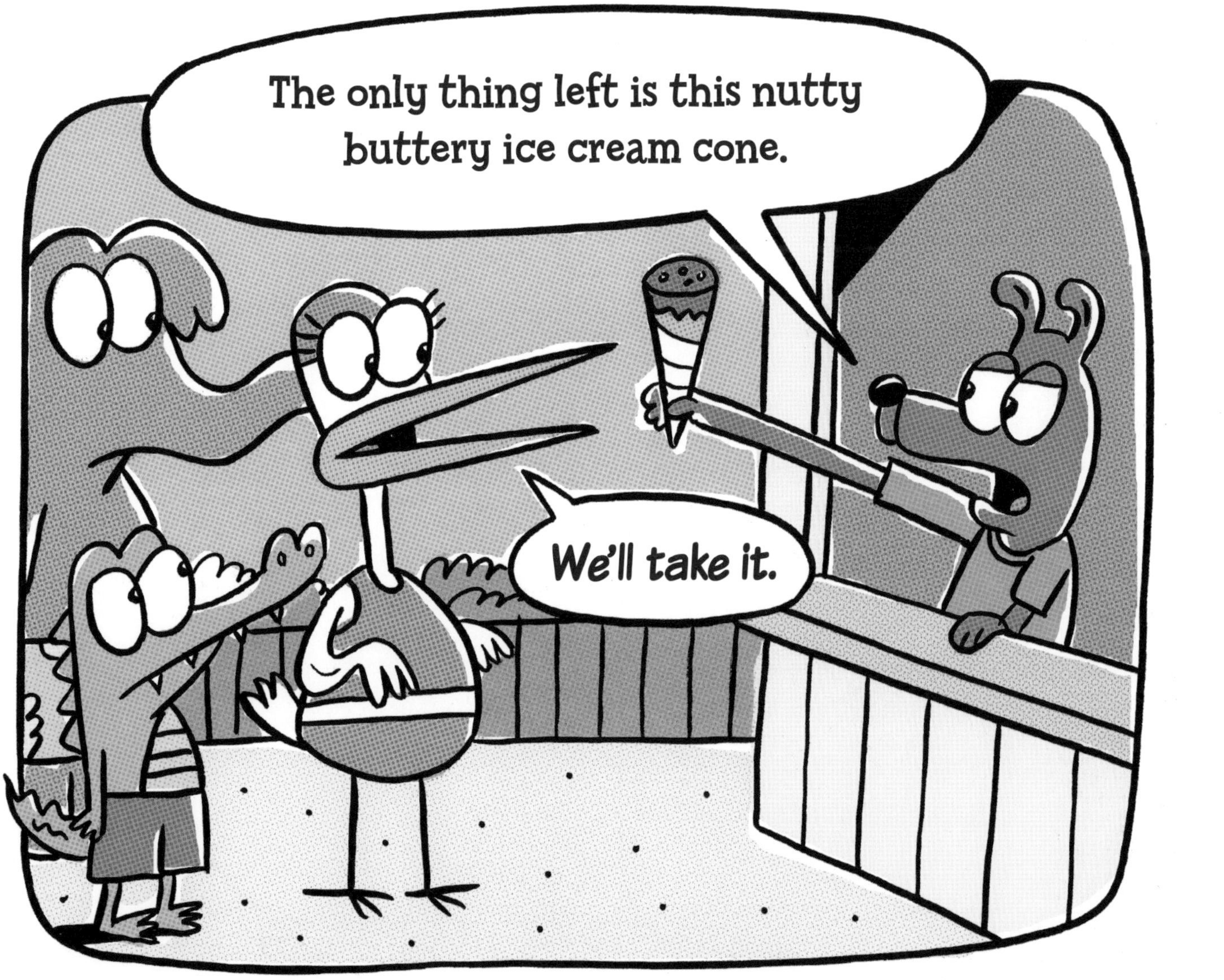
The only thing left is this nutty buttery ice cream cone.
We'll take it.

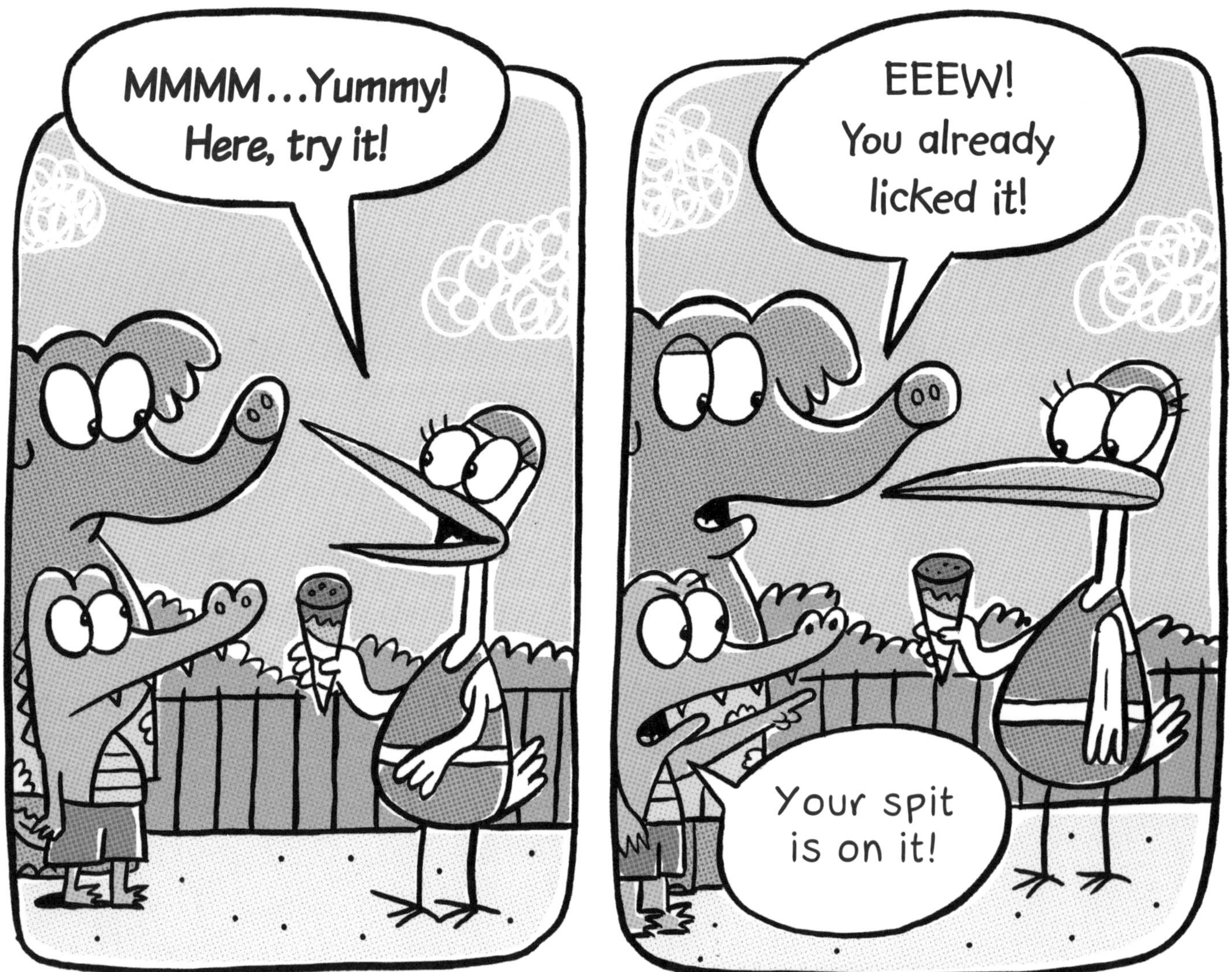
MMMM...Yummy! Here, try it!
EEEW! You already licked it!
Your spit is on it!

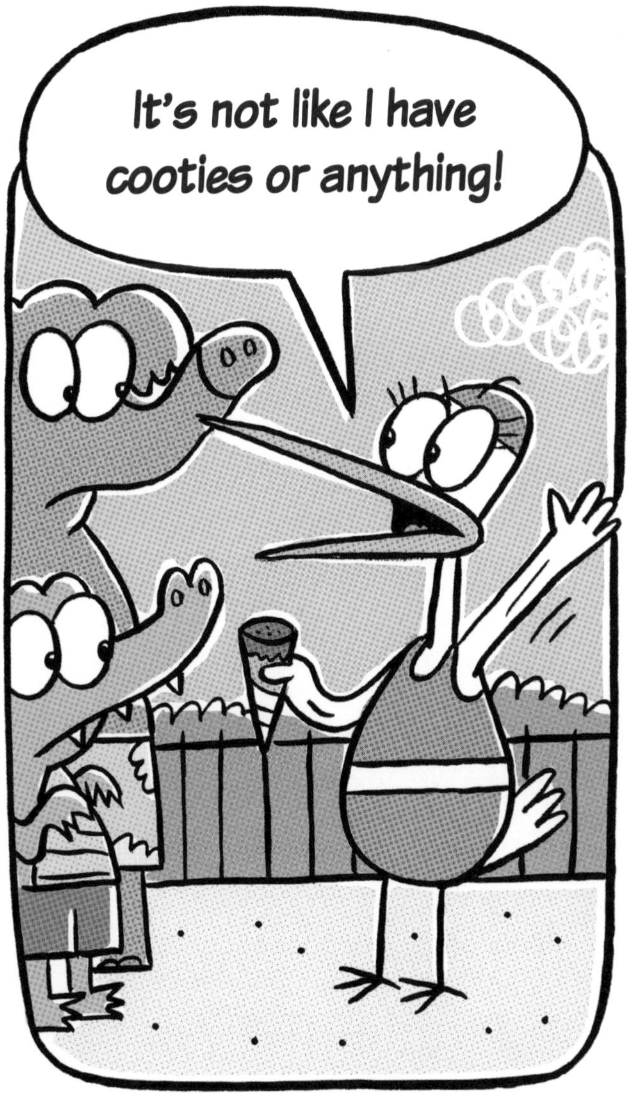
It's not like I have cooties or anything!

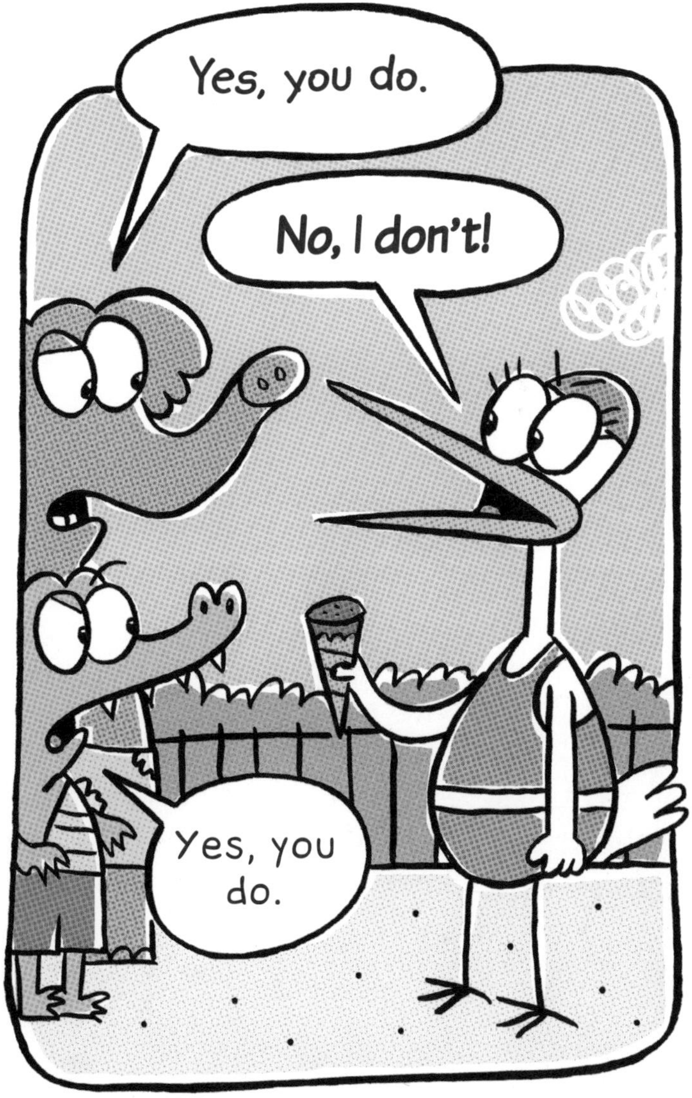
Yes, you do.
No, I don't!
Yes, you do.

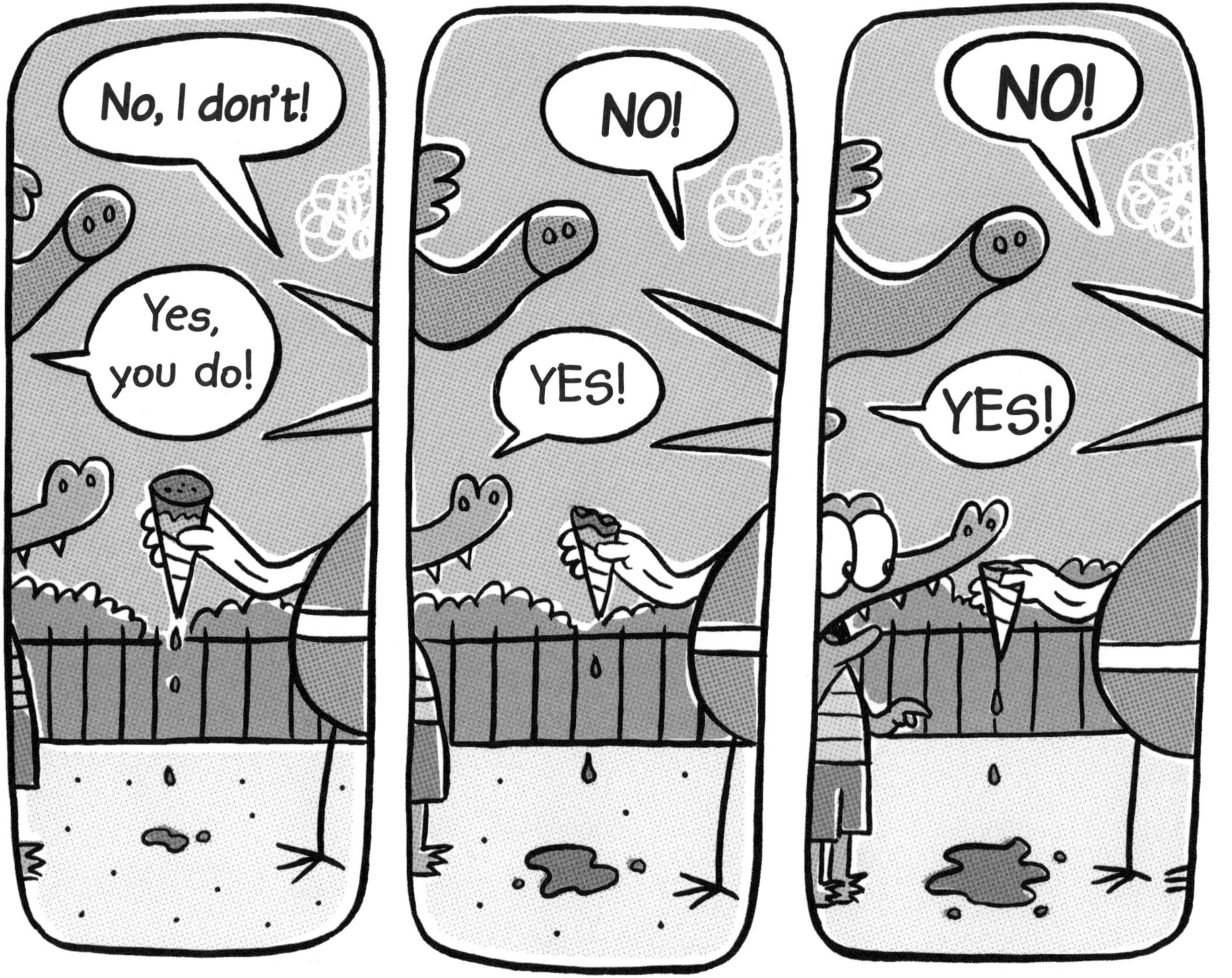
No, I don't!
Yes, you do!
NO!
YES!
NO!
YES!

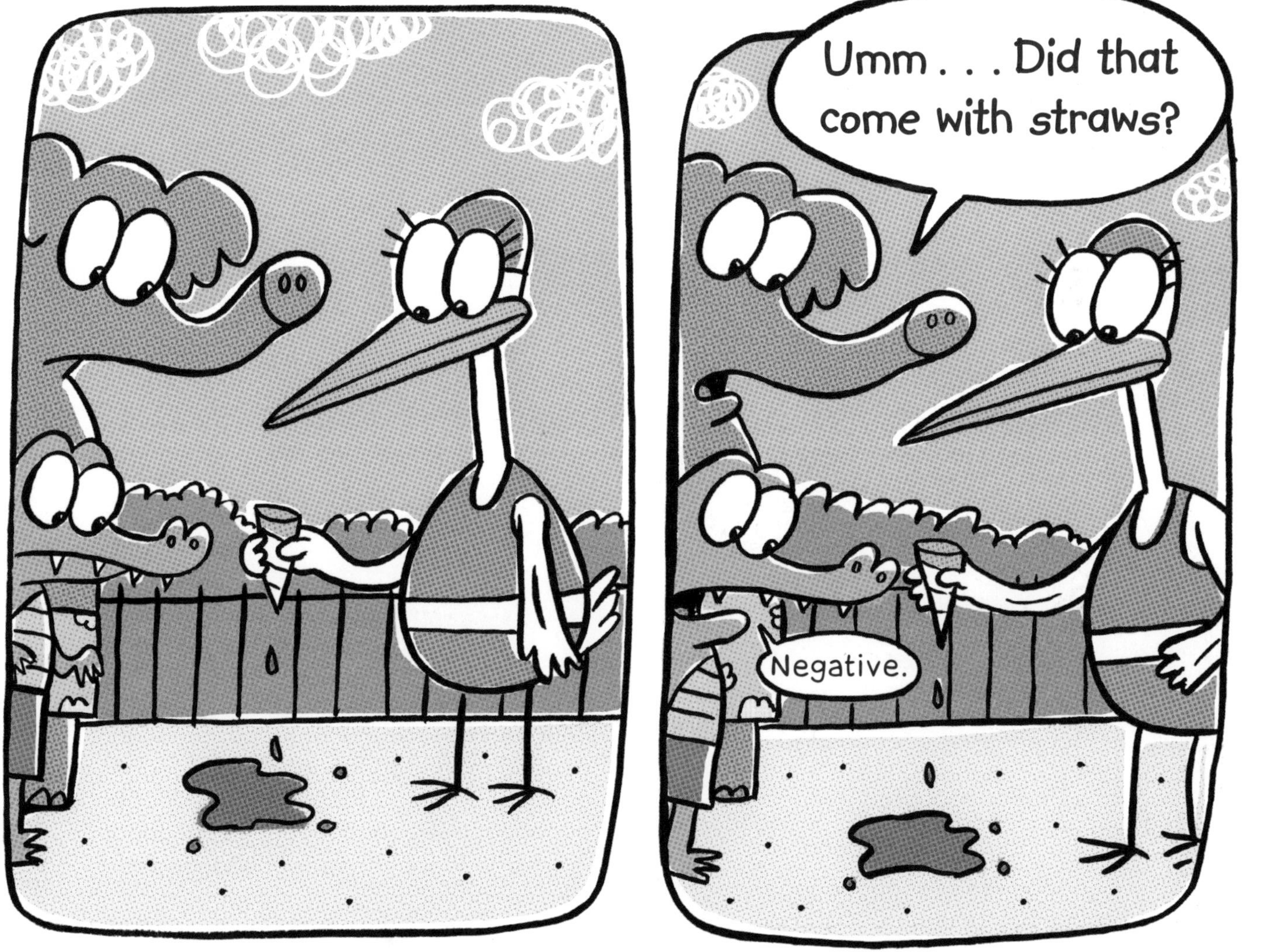
Umm . . . Did that come with straws?
Negative.

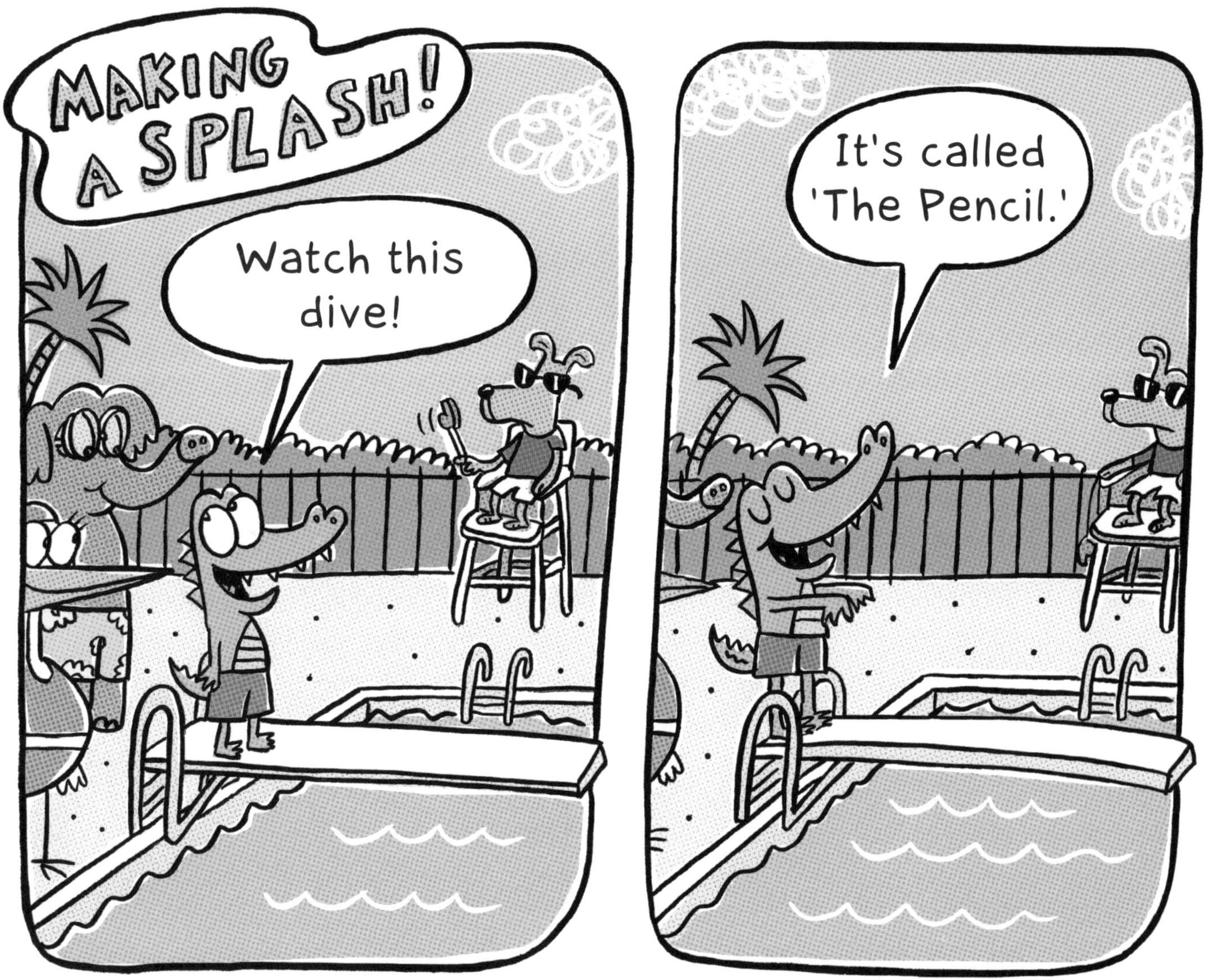
MAKING A SPLASH!
Watch this dive!
It's called 'The Pencil.'

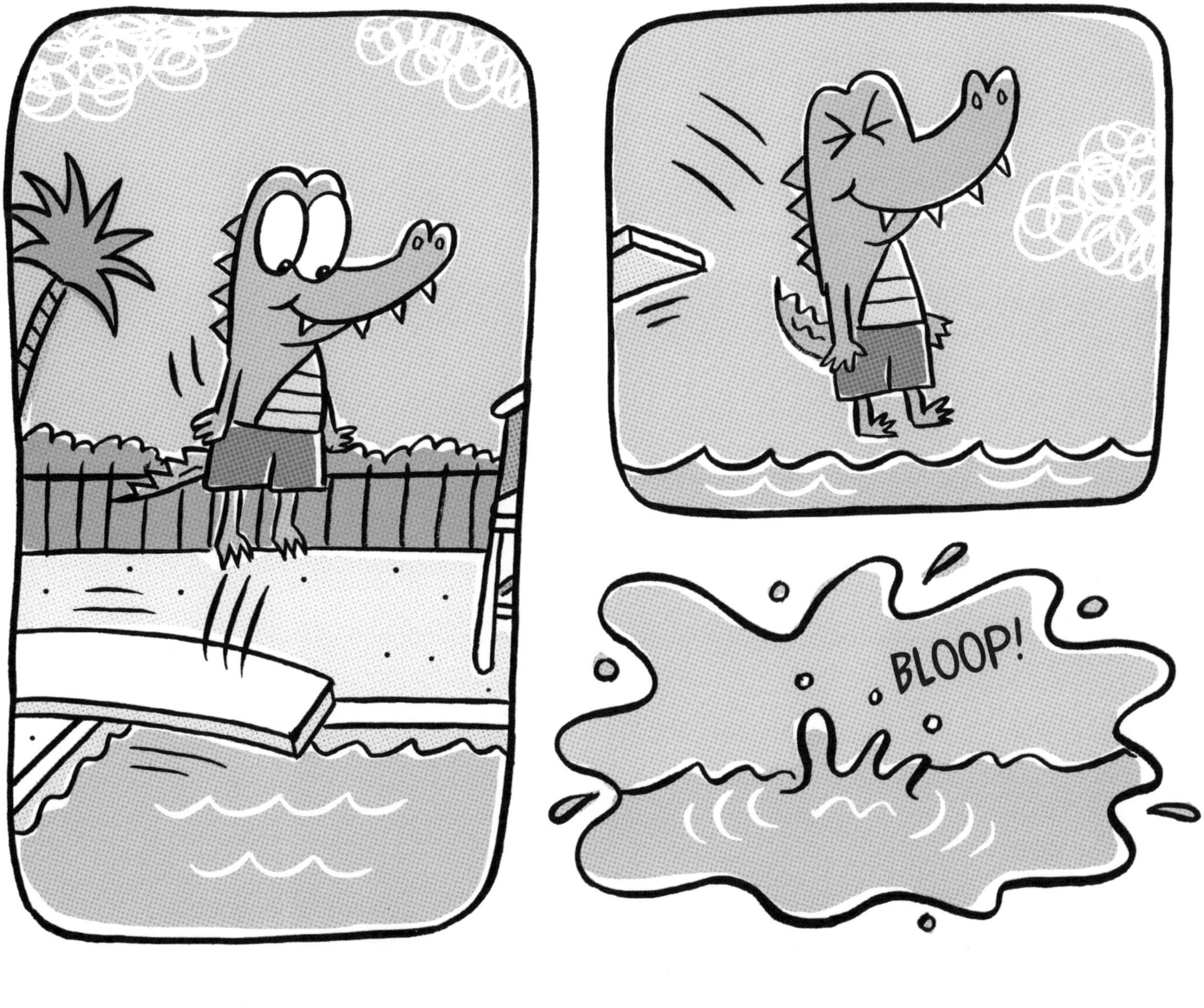
BLOOP!

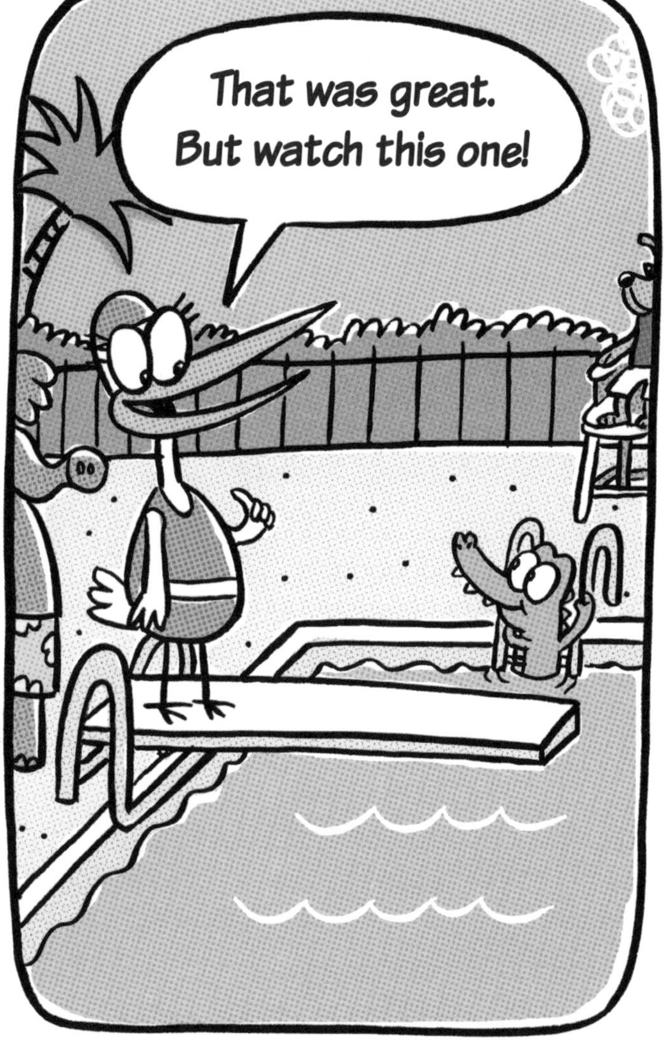
That was great.
But watch this one!

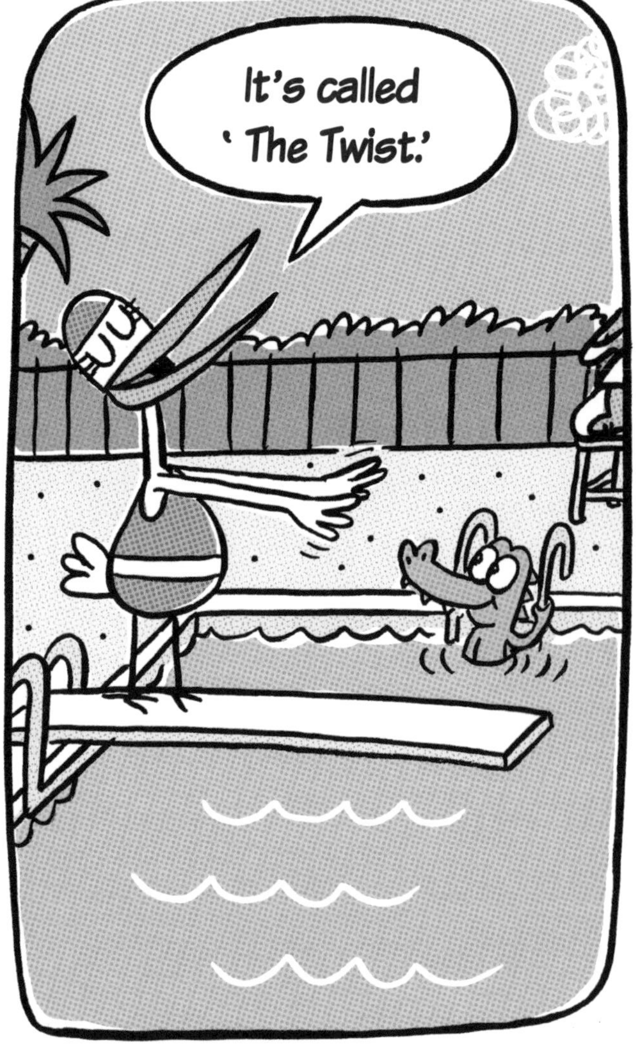
It's called
'The Twist.'

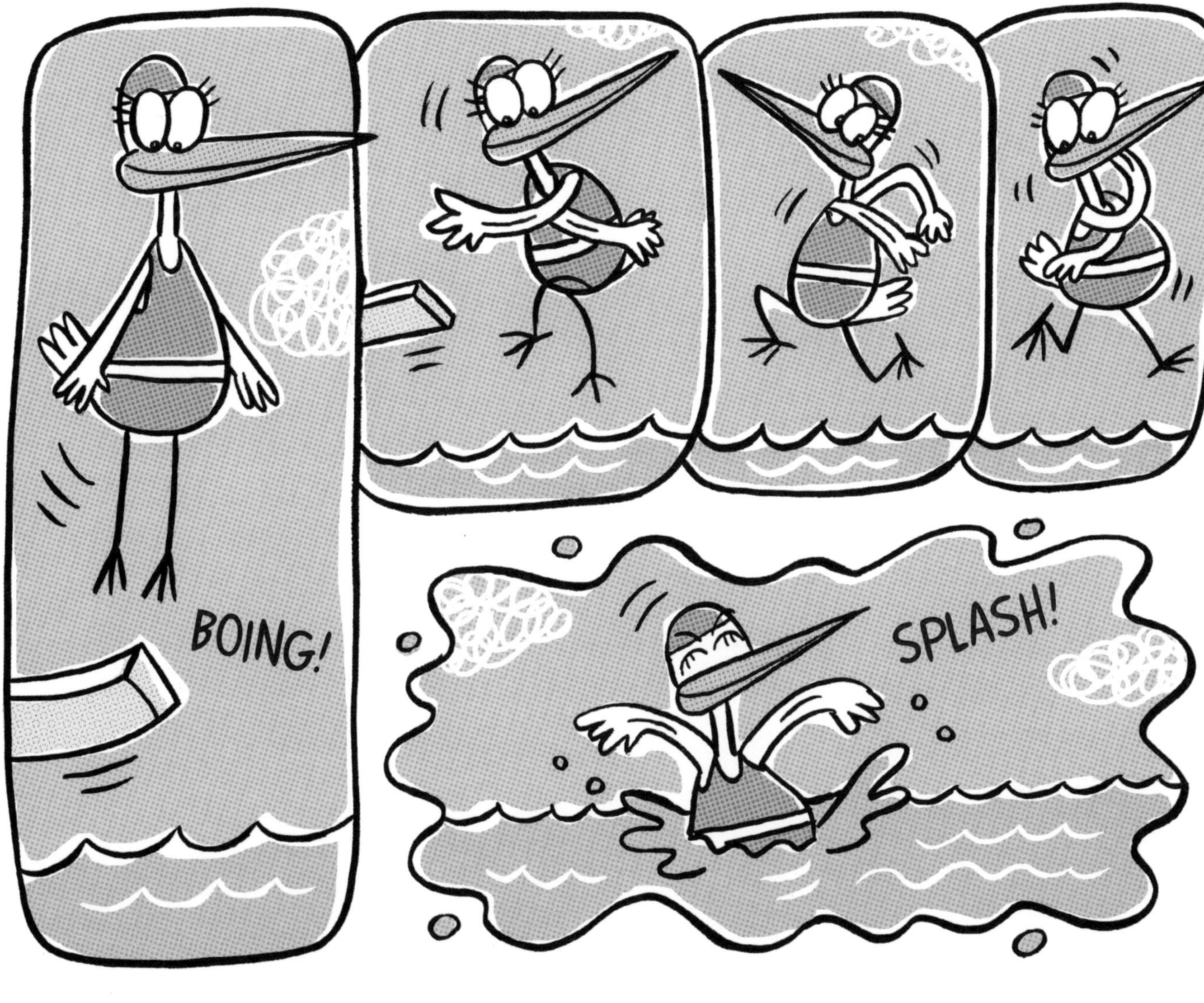
BOING!
SPLASH!

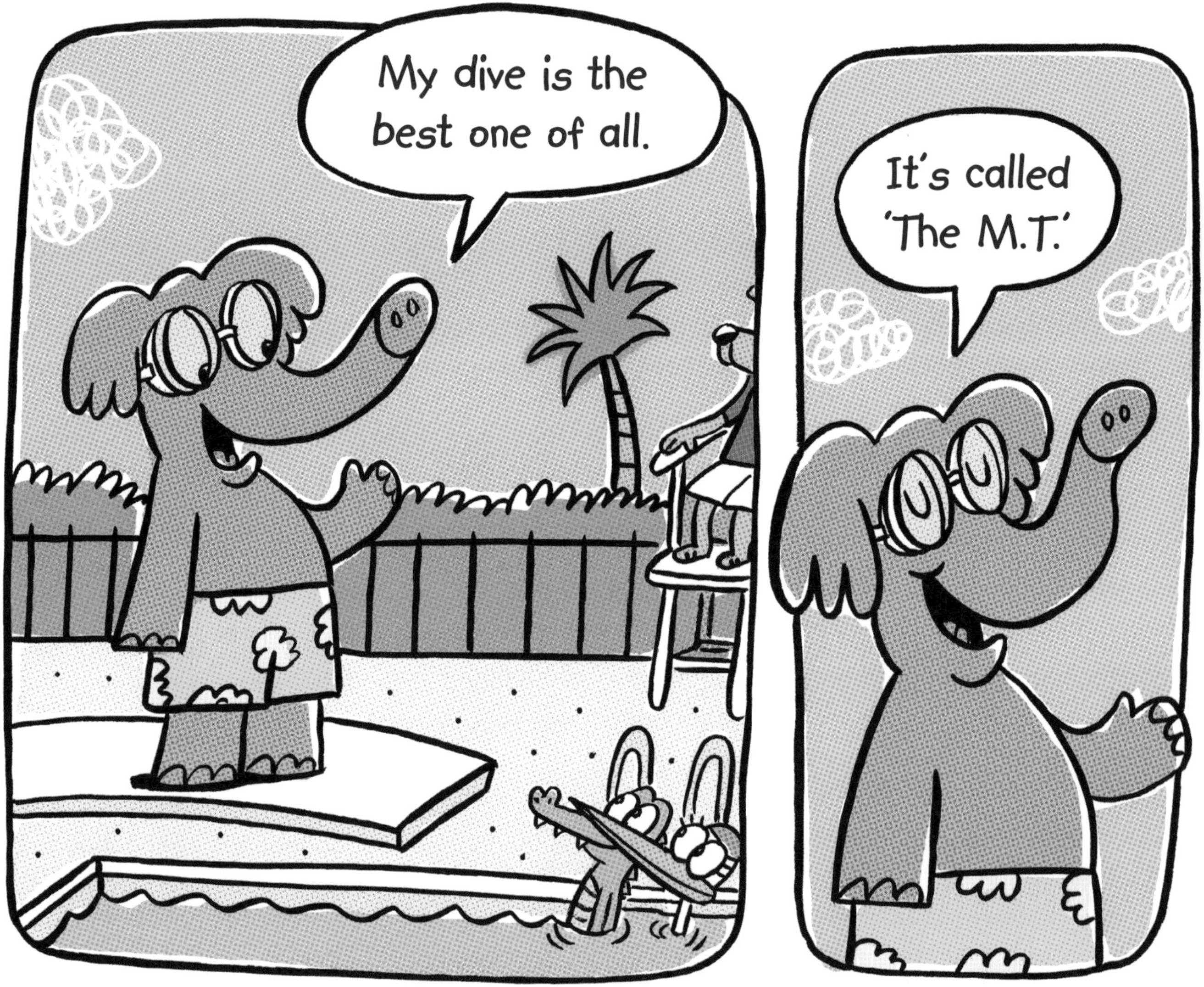
My dive is the best one of all.
It's called 'The M.T.'

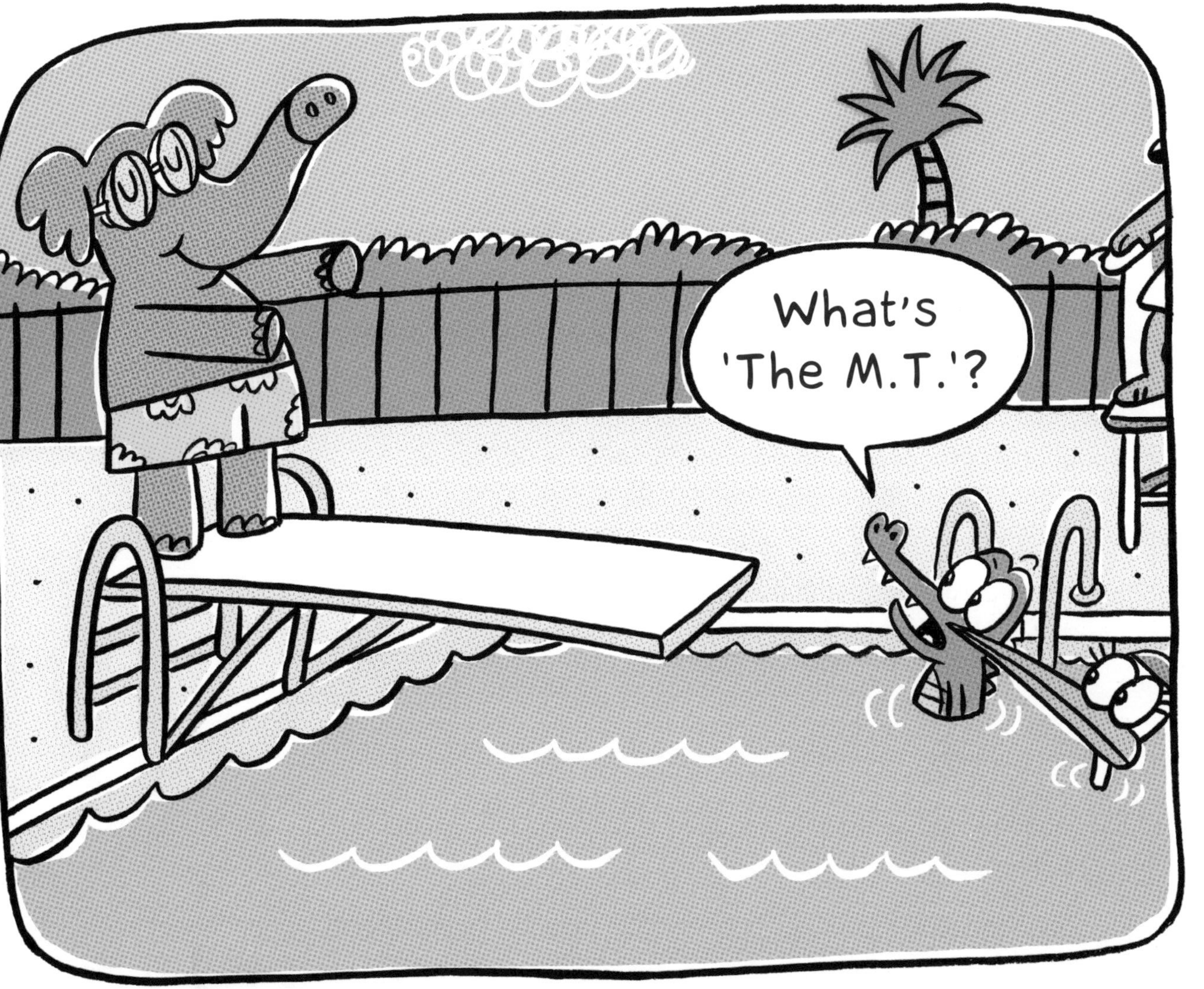
What's 'The M.T.'?

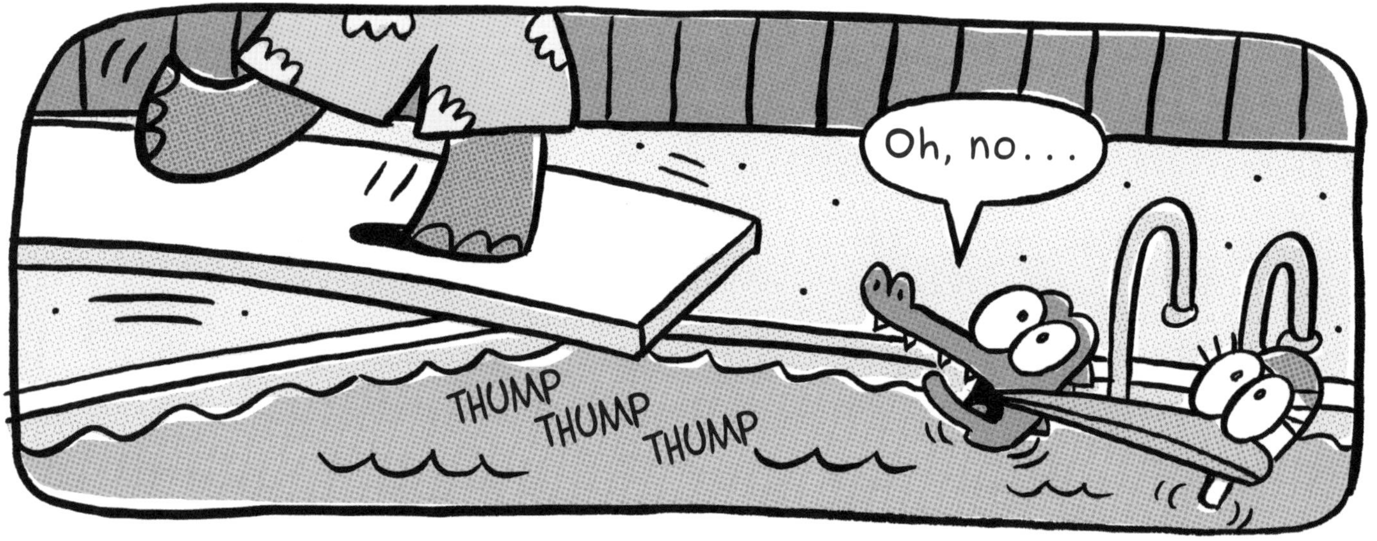
Oh, no. . .
THUMP
THUMP
THUMP

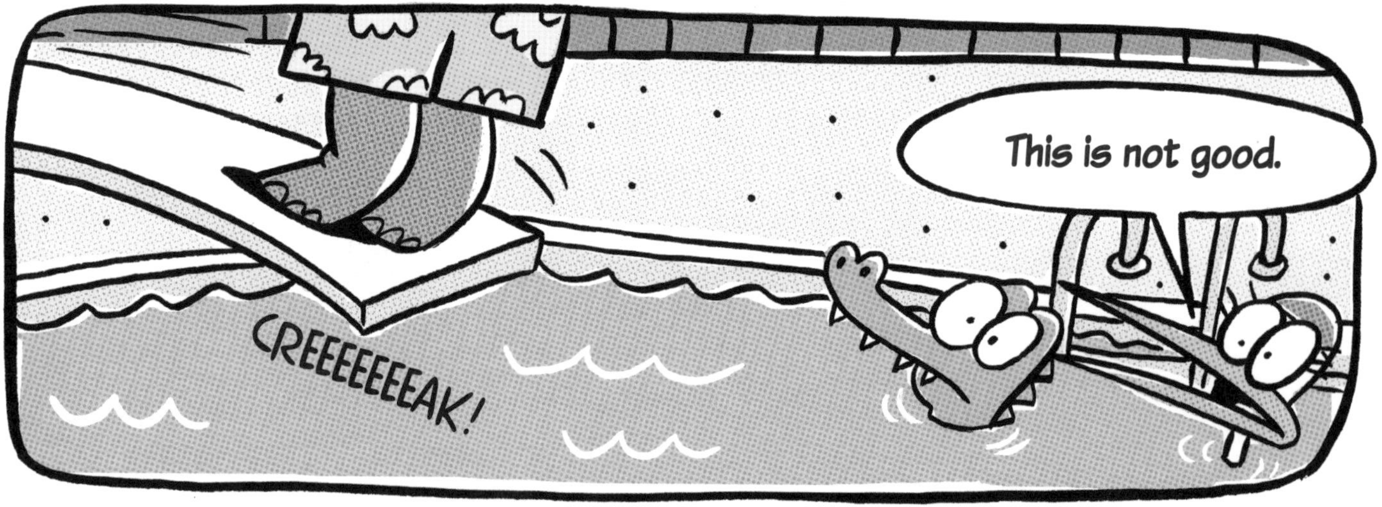
CREEEEEEEAK!
This is not good.

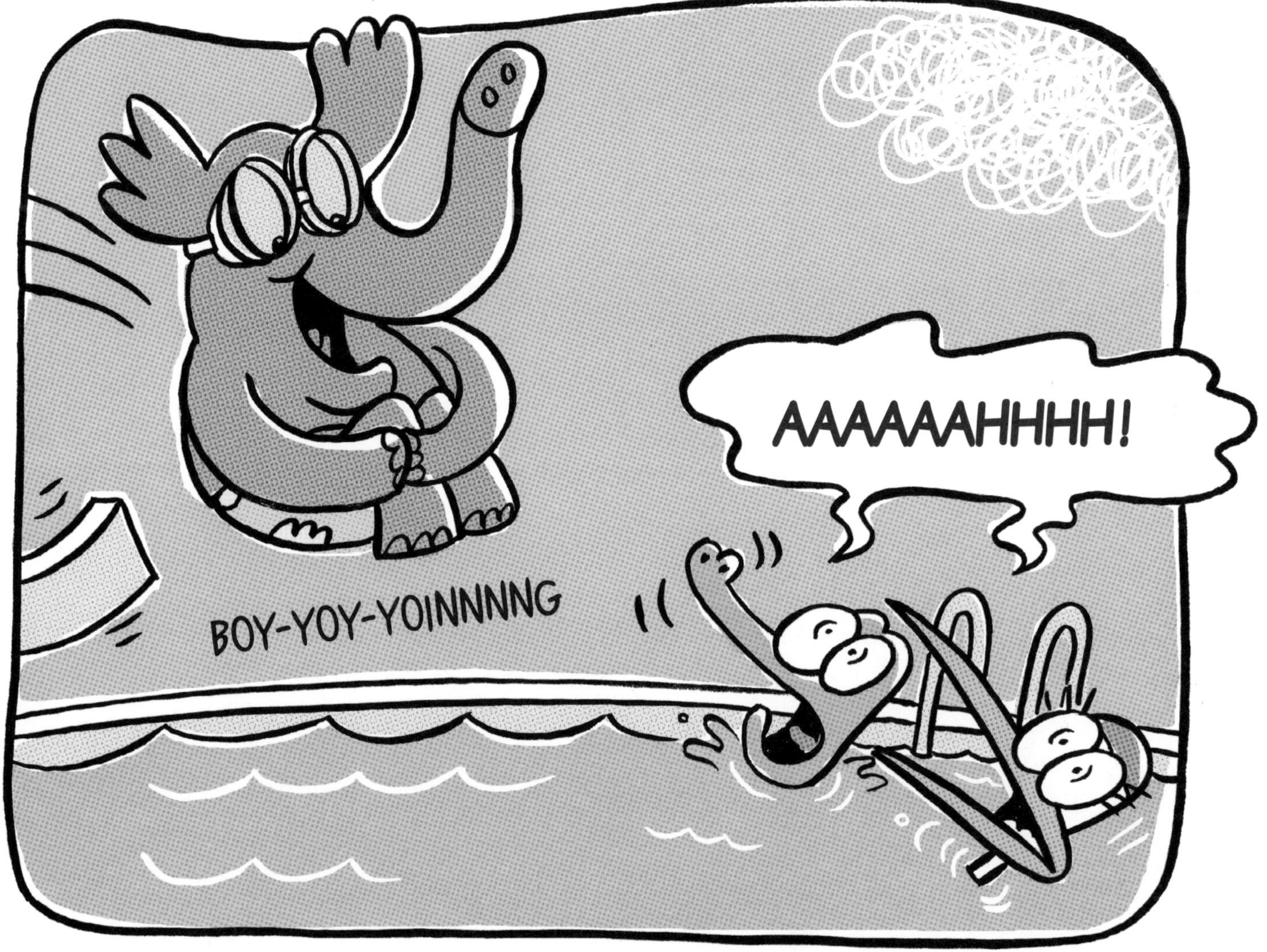
BOY-YOY-YOINNNNG
AAAAAAHHHH!

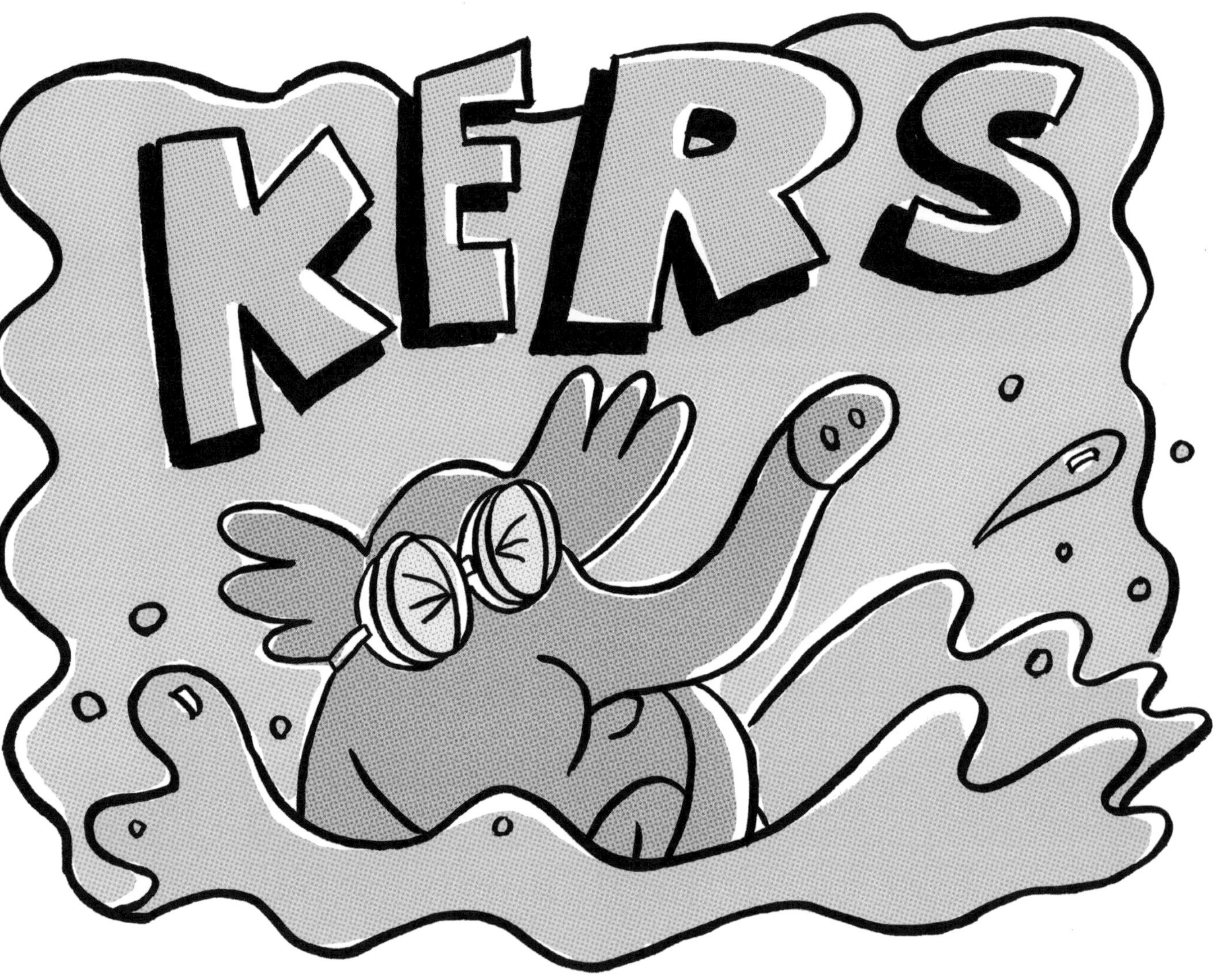
KERS

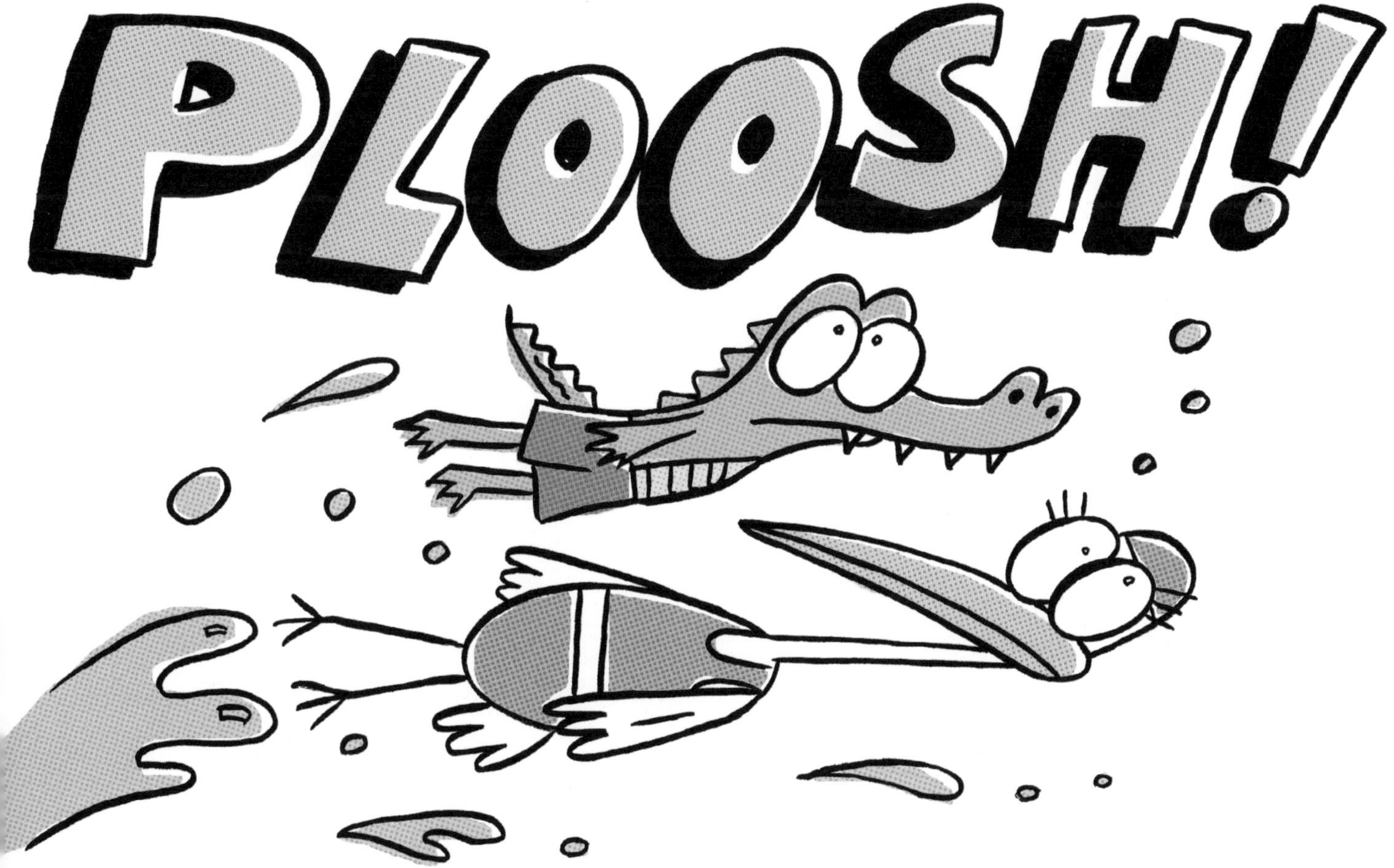
PLOOSH!

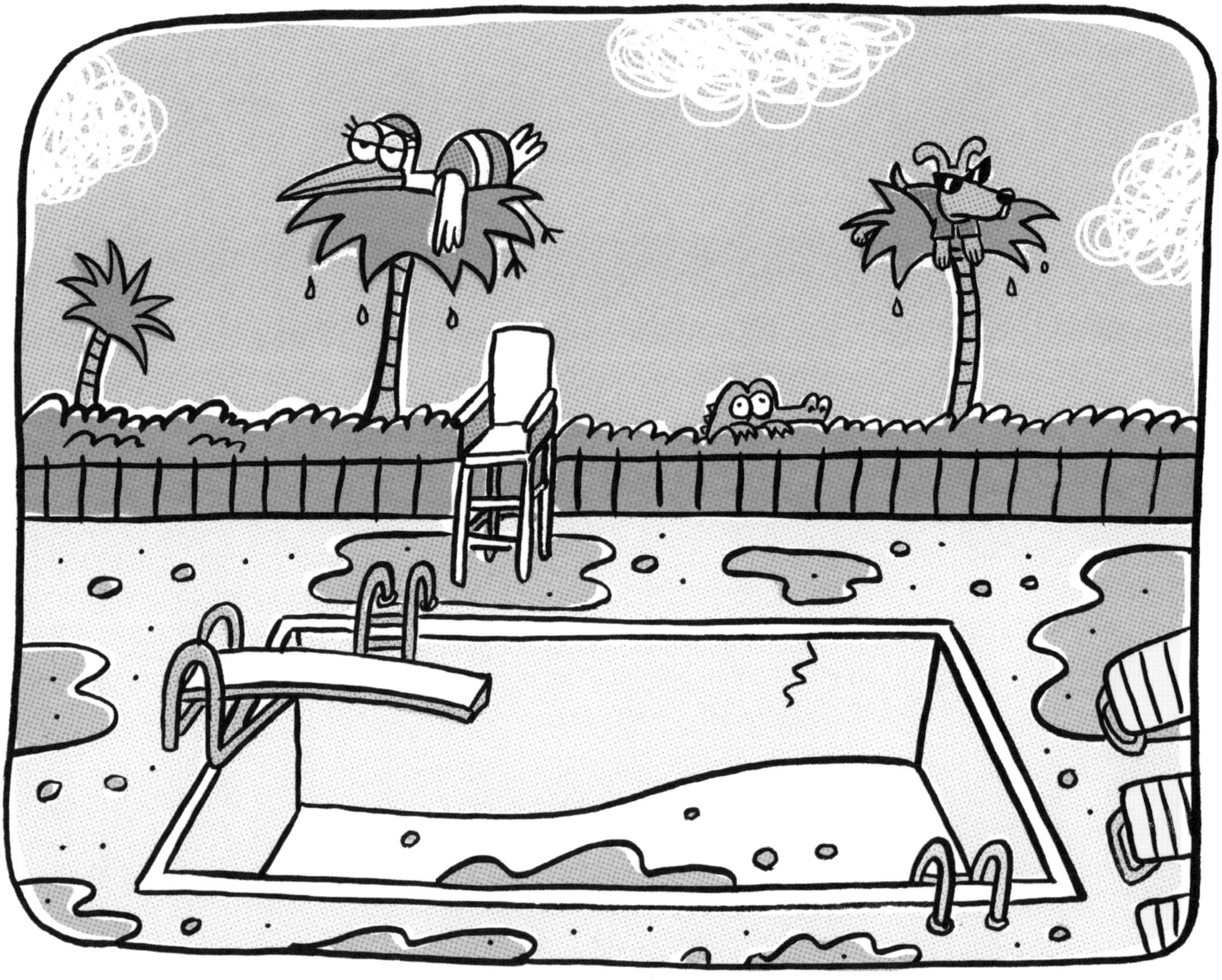

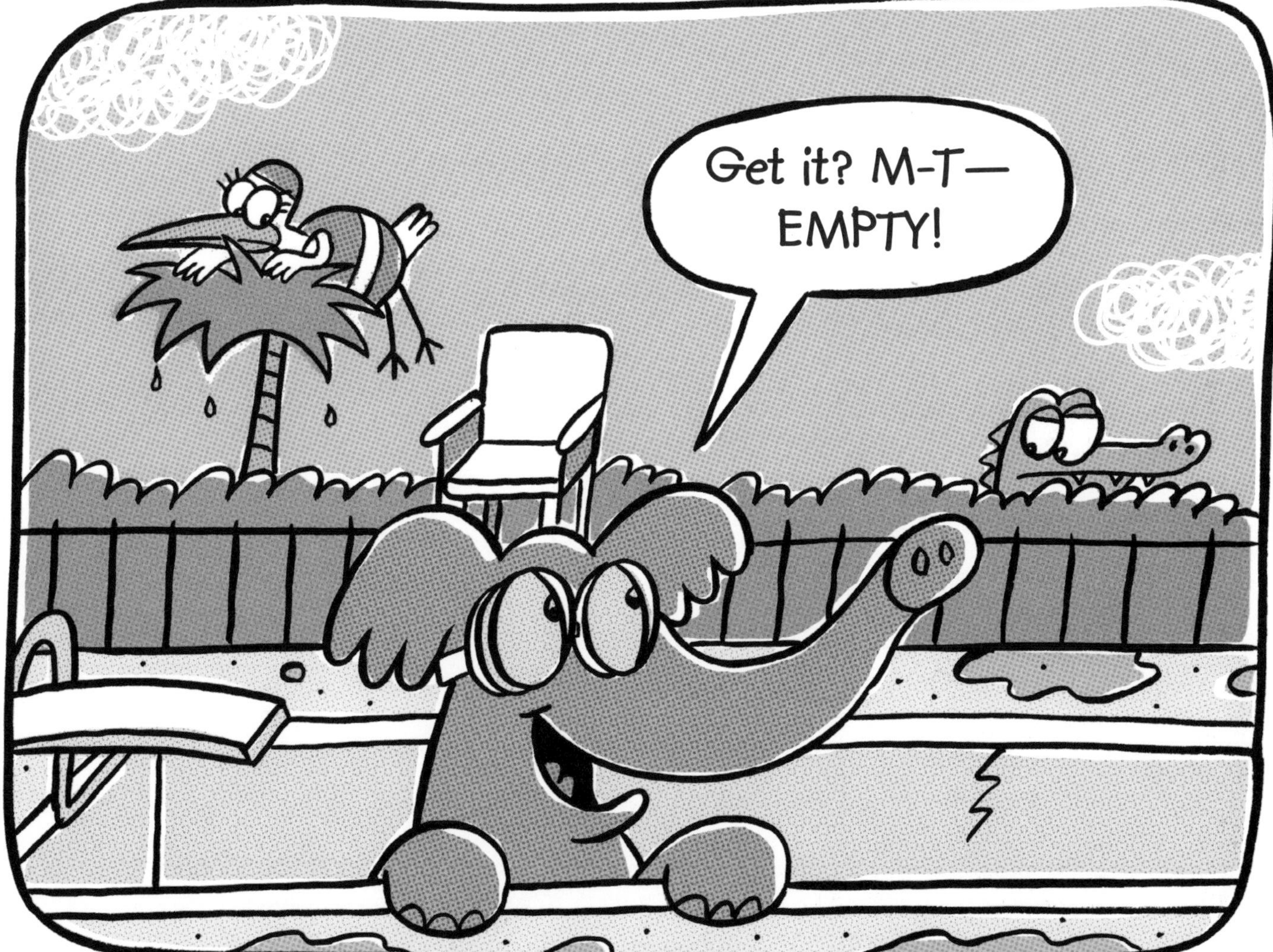
Get it? M-T—
EMPTY!

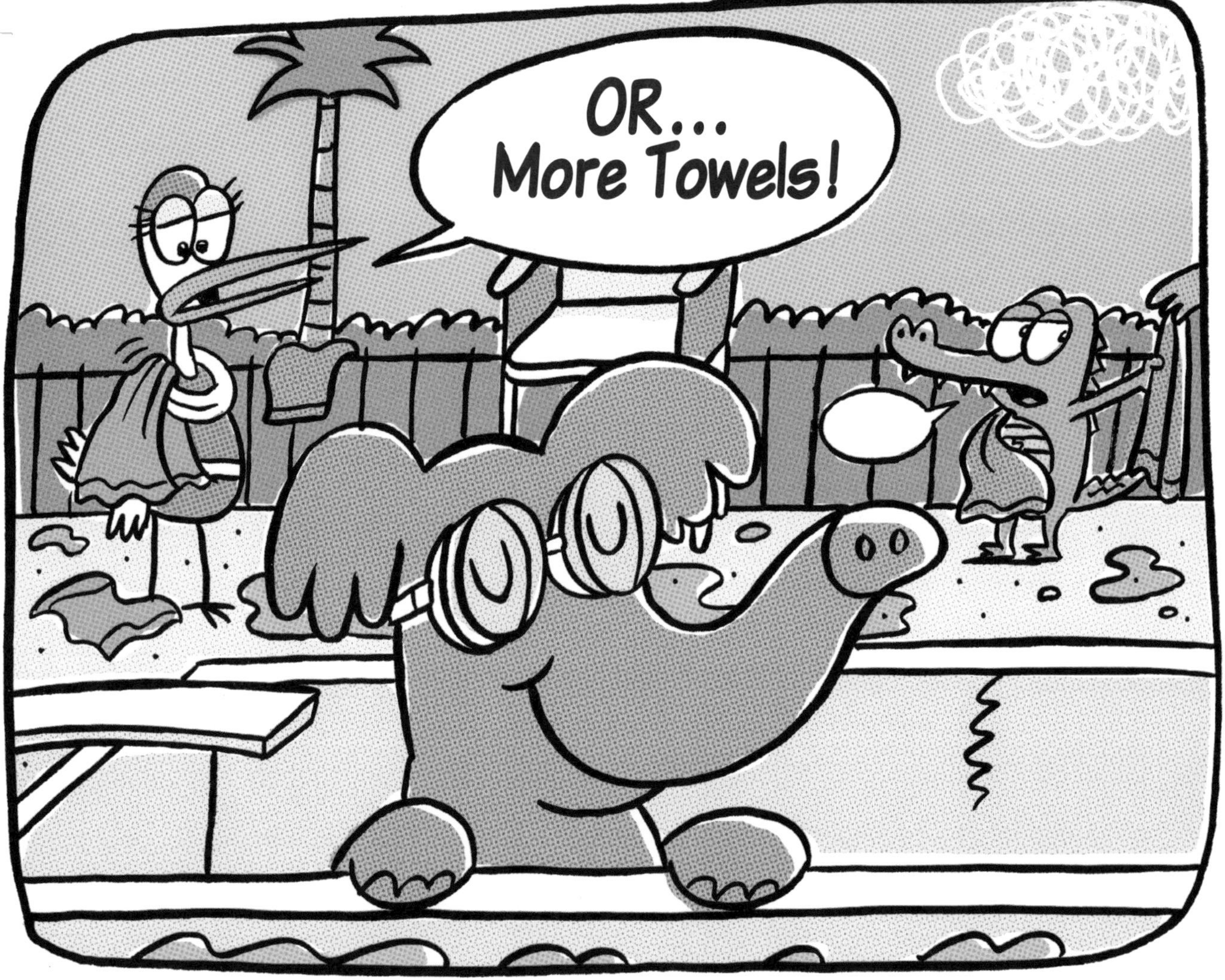
OR...
More Towels!

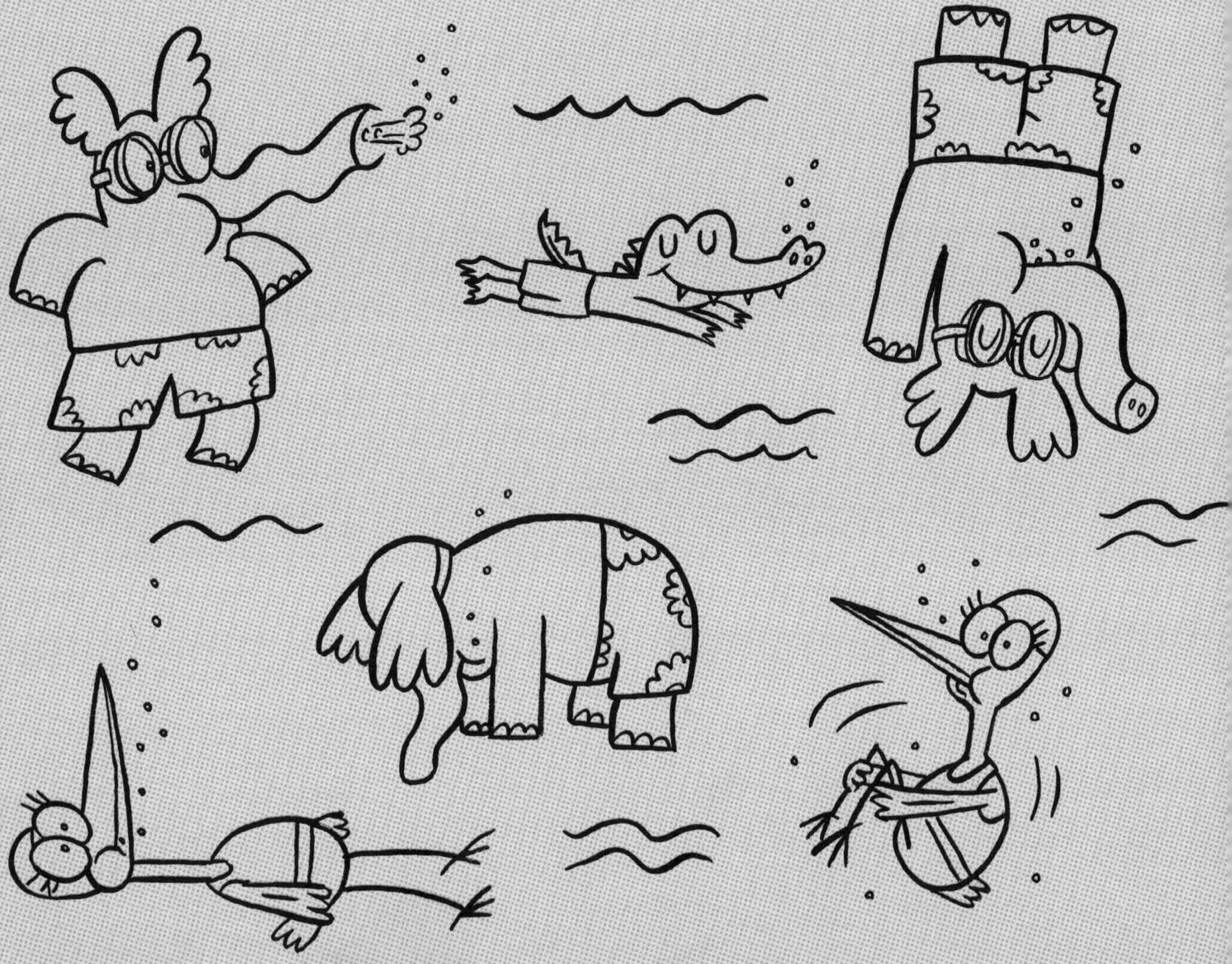